In the Next Room
or
the vibrator play

by Sarah Ruhl

A SAMUEL FRENCH ACTING EDITION

SAMUEL FRENCH

FOUNDED 1830

NEW YORK HOLLYWOOD LONDON TORONTO

SAMUELFRENCH.COM

Copyright © 2010 by Sarah Ruhl

ALL RIGHTS RESERVED

Art copyright © James McMullan
Used by the permission of Pippin Properties, Inc.

CAUTION: Professionals and amateurs are hereby warned that *IN THE NEXT ROOM, OR THE VIBRATOR PLAY* is subject to a Licensing Fee. It is fully protected under the copyright laws of the United States of America, the British Commonwealth, including Canada, and all other countries of the Copyright Union. All rights, including professional, amateur, motion picture, recitation, lecturing, public reading, radio broadcasting, television and the rights of translation into foreign languages are strictly reserved. In its present form the play is dedicated to the reading public only.

The amateur live stage performance rights to *IN THE NEXT ROOM, OR THE VIBRATOR PLAY* are controlled exclusively by Samuel French, Inc., and licensing arrangements and performance licenses must be secured well in advance of presentation. PLEASE NOTE that amateur Licensing Fees are set upon application in accordance with your producing circumstances. When applying for a licensing quotation and a performance license please give us the number of performances intended, dates of production, your seating capacity and admission fee. Licensing Fees are payable one week before the opening performance of the play to Samuel French, Inc., at 45 W. 25th Street, New York, NY 10010.

Licensing Fee of the required amount must be paid whether the play is presented for charity or gain and whether or not admission is charged.

Stock licensing fees quoted upon application to Samuel French, Inc.

For all other rights than those stipulated above, apply to: Bret Adams, 448 West 44th Street, New York, NY 10036 Attn: Bruce Ostler.

Particular emphasis is laid on the question of amateur or professional readings, permission and terms for which must be secured in writing from Samuel French, Inc.

Copying from this book in whole or in part is strictly forbidden by law, and the right of performance is not transferable.

Whenever the play is produced the following notice must appear on all programs, printing and advertising for the play: "Produced by special arrangement with Samuel French, Inc."

Due authorship credit must be given on all programs, printing and advertising for the play.

ISBN 978-0-573-69813-2   Printed in U.S.A.   #29515

No one shall commit or authorize any act or omission by which the copyright of, or the right to copyright, this play may be impaired.

No one shall make any changes in this play for the purpose of production.

Publication of this play does not imply availability for performance. Both amateurs and professionals considering a production are strongly advised in their own interests to apply to Samuel French, Inc., for written permission before starting rehearsals, advertising, or booking a theatre.

No part of this book may be reproduced, stored in a retrieval system, or transmitted in any form, by any means, now known or yet to be invented, including mechanical, electronic, photocopying, recording, videotaping, or otherwise, without the prior written permission of the publisher.

MUSIC USE NOTE

Licensees are solely responsible for obtaining formal written permission from copyright owners to use copyrighted music in the performance of this play and are strongly cautioned to do so. If no such permission is obtained by the licensee, then the licensee must use only original music that the licensee owns and controls. Licensees are solely responsible and liable for all music clearances and shall indemnify the copyright owners of the play and their licensing agent, Samuel French, Inc., against any costs, expenses, losses and liabilities arising from the use of music by licensees.

To obtain the original compositions of the piano music and songs used in the play, contact composer Jonathan Bell at www.jonathanbellmusic.com

IMPORTANT BILLING AND CREDIT REQUIREMENTS

All producers of *IN THE NEXT ROOM, OR THE VIBRATOR PLAY must* give credit to the Author of the Play in all programs distributed in connection with performances of the Play, and in all instances in which the title of the Play appears for the purposes of advertising, publicizing or otherwise exploiting the Play and/or a production. The name of the Author *must* appear on a separate line on which no other name appears, immediately following the title and *must* appear in size of type not less than fifty percent of the size of the title type.

In addition the following credit *must* be given in all programs and publicity information distributed in association with this piece, on title page of program and billing page of the publication and in all advertising of ½ page or larger:

Original Broadway Production by Lincoln Center Theater New York City, 2009

**IN THE NEXT ROOM *or the vibrator play*
was originally commissioned and produced by
Berkeley Repertory Theatre, Berkeley, CA
Tony Taccone, Artistic Director / Susan Medak, Managing Director**

And on a separate line and less prominently shall read the following additional credit:

**IN THE NEXT ROOM *or the vibrator play*
was developed at New Dramatists**

IN THE NEXT ROOM OR THE VIBRATOR PLAY was first produced by the Berkeley Repertory Theater, at the Berkeley Rep Roda Theater in Berkeley, California in Feburary, 2009. The performance was directed The performance was directed by Les Waters, with sets by Annie Smart, costumes by David Zinn, lighting by Russell H. Champa, sound by Bray Poor, and music by Jonathan Bell. The production stage manager was Michael Suenkel. The cast was as follows:

CATHERINE GIVINGS . . . . Hannah Cabell
DR. GIVINGS . . . . .Paul Niebanck
SABRINA DALDRY . . . . Maria Dizzia
ANNIE . . . . Stacy Ross
LEO IRVING . . . . Joaquín Torres
ELIZABETH . . . . .Melle Powers
MR. DALDRY . . . . John Leonard Thompson

IN THE NEXT ROOM OR THE VIBRATOR PLAY was produced by the Lincoln Center Theater, under the direction of André Bishop and Bernard Gersten, at the Lyceum Theater in November, 2009. The performance was directed by Les Waters, with sets by Annie Smart, costumes by David Zinn, lighting by Russell H. Champa, sound by Bray Poor, and music by Jonathan Bell. The cast was as follows:

CATHERINE GIVINGS . . . . .Laura Benanti
DR. GIVINGS . . . . .Michael Cerveris
SABRINA DALDRY . . . . Maria Dizzia
ANNIE . . . . Wendy Rich Stetson
LEO IRVING . . . . Chandler Williams
ELIZABETH . . . . Quincy Tyler Bernstine
MR. DALDRY . . . . Thomas Jay Ryan

IN THE NEXT ROOM OR THE VIBRATOR PLAY was nominated for the 2010 Tony® Award for Best Play and was selected as a Finalist for the 2010 Pulitzer Prize.

On the stage:

A piano.
Closed curtains.
Knick knacks.
One chaise.
A birdcage.
A pram/bassinette.
A rocking chair.
Sumptuous rugs, sumptuous wallpaper.
Many electrical lamps, and one particularly beautiful one,
with green glass.

Next to the living room, a private doctor's room, otherwise known
as an operating theater.
The relationship between the living room and the operating theater
is all important in the design, as things happen simultaneously
in the living room and operating theater.
In the operating theater, a medical table covered with a sheet.
A basin for washing hands.
Several vibrators.
And an outlet, to plug in electrical apparatus.
One exit, in the operating room, to an unseen room (the doctor's private study) and one exit to the living room, which has an exit to an
unseen nursery and to the outdoors.

One might consider, rather than recorded sound,
using only the live piano if one of the actors is good
at playing piano.
One might consider, rather than the usual lighting instruments,
something ancient.
That is to say – in a play hovering at the dawn of electricity –
how should the theater itself feel?
Terribly technological or terribly primitive or neither –
At any rate, let the use of technology feel like a choice.

Personages:

DR. GIVINGS – A man in his forties, a specialist in gynecological and hysterical disorders.

CATHERINE GIVINGS – His wife, a woman in her late twenties.

SABRINA DALDRY – His patient, a woman in her early thirties.

ANNIE – A woman in her late thirties, Dr. Giving's midwife assitant.

LEO IRVING – Dr. Giving's other patient, a Englishman in his twenties or thirties.

ELIZABETH – An African-American woman in her early thirties. A wet-nurse by default.

MR. DALDRY – Sabrina Daldry's husband, a man in his forties or fifties.

* * *

Place:

A prosperous spa town outside of New York City,
perhaps Saratoga Springs

* * *

Time:

The dawn of the age of electricity; and after the Civil War; circa 1880s

* * *

PLAYWRIGHT'S NOTES

Be sure to rehearse with a close approximation of the costumes you will be using (with the proper buttons and corsets) as the timing of dressing and undressing is all-important when synchronizing with the dialogue.

During simultaneous action, actors should never appear to be still or "waiting" for the other room to finish.

I am indebted to the book *The Technology of Orgasm* by Rachel P. Maines for inspiration. Thanks to Luke Walden for putting me on to it. Another debt is due to *AC/DC: The Savage Tale of the First Standards War,* by Tom McHichol, for thoughts on electricity. Thanks to my husband for finding it for me. A final debt is due to *A Social History of Wet Nursing in America: from Breast to Bottle* by Janet Golden and *Parallel Lives: Five Victorian Marriages* by Phyllis Rose.

Astericks indicate quotations from primary historical sources.

Things that seem impossibly strange in the following play are all true—such as the Chattanooga Vibrator—and the vagaries of wet-nursing. Things that seem commonplace are all my own invention.

To my husband. For the garden on Hope Street.

Act I

First Scene

Mrs. Givings turns on her electric lamp.
She shows it to her baby.
Meanwhile, in the operating theater,
Annie changes the sheets on the bed
and cleans medical equipment in the sink.

MRS. GIVINGS. Look baby, it's light! No candle, no rusty tool to snuff it out, but light, pure light, straight from man's imagination into our living room. On, off, on, off, on –

She turns it off and on.
Dr. Givings enters.
He walks through the space
without saying hello to his wife.
She watches him. After he exits:

MRS. GIVINGS. Hello.

Dr. Givings re-enters.

DR. GIVINGS. Sorry. Hello, darling.

He exits again.

MRS. GIVINGS. *(to the baby)* We'll find a nice nurse for you, won't we? A nice wet nurse with lots of healthy milk. Your father put an advertisement in the paper and we'll get lots of replies today. My milk is not filling you up, is it? Are you less fat today, darling? Are your cheeks less fat?

She is near tears. She recovers.

I'll find you a nurse who hasn't a child of her own. Not that I hope to find a nurse with a dead baby for that

9

MRS. GIVINGS. *(cont.)* is tragic nothing is more tragic oh it hurts me here to think it – you in your pram not moving – but I suppose if I am to find a childless nurse with milk to spare, her baby must be dead, and recently dead, oh dear. I don't like to think of that.

Dr. Givings enters again.

DR. GIVINGS. I have a new patient who might ring the doorbell any second. If she arrives, would you please let Annie answer the door.

The doorbell rings.

DR. GIVINGS. Her nerves are terribly raw and it might throw off the entire clinical balance for her to meet you and the baby.

The doorbell rings.

DR. GIVINGS. Please hide. *(Shouting to his midwife)* Annie!

Mrs. Givings hides behind a piano.
Dr. Givings runs out with the pram.
Annie answers the door.

ANNIE. Hello, you must be Mr. and Mrs. Daldry, please come in.

Mr. and Mrs. Daldry enter.
Mrs. Daldry is fragile and ethereal.
Her face is covered by a veil attached to a hat.
She leans heavily on her husband's arm.

ANNIE. This way, let me show you to the operating theater –

Mrs. Daldry startles.

ANNIE. Well let's just call it the next room for now, shall we, don't be nervous,

MRS. DALDRY. Shall I just put your hat here?

Mrs. Daldry shakes her head.

MR. DALDRY. She's very sensitive to light.

ANNIE. Of course. Right this way.

Annie turns off the electric lamp.
She leads them to the office.

Mrs. Daldry arrives in the operating theater. Dr. Givings enters from the living room.

DR. GIVINGS. So nice to meet you, Mrs. Daldry, Mr. Daldry. Shall I take your coat?

Mrs. Daldry shakes her head.

MR. DALDRY. She's very sensitive to cold.

DR. GIVINGS. I see. Well, have a seat. Sensitive to light, sensitive to cold –

A baby's cry is heard.

MRS. DALDRY. Oh, is there a baby here? I didn't know there was a new baby. How wonderful for you.

DR. GIVINGS. Yes. Could you shut the door please Annie?

She does so.
Then Annie sits invisibly in the corner, listening.
Dr. Givings sits and takes out his note-pad.
Mrs. Givings, meanwhile, in the next room, has heard the baby cry.
She sneaks out and exits to the nursery.

DR. GIVINGS. What other symptoms is your wife suffering from?

MR. DALDRY. I find her weeping at odd moments during the day, muttering about green curtains or some such nonsense.

DR. GIVINGS. Is it nonsense, Mrs. Daldry?

MRS. DALDRY. I suppose it is. The green curtains give me terrible head-ache. The color. Old ghosts in the dark.

Mr. Daldry gives Dr. Givings a pointed look.

DR. GIVINGS. Tell me more about the curtains, would you?

MRS. DALDRY. The house where I grew up my mother would wash the curtains every week, she beat them with a stick, and there were no ghosts in them. There was a beautiful view of a grape arbor and when the curtains were cleaned you could see right through to the grapes, you could almost watch them growing,

MRS. GIVINGS. *(cont.)* they got so plump in the autumn. My mother would make loads of jam – my mother was not a nervous or excitable woman. It was jam, it was laughing, and long walks out of doors. We haven't a grape arbor here – I am full of digressions these days Dr. Givings – but the point is I haven't the strength to wash the curtains every week and beat the ghosts out of them. You think I am talking like a madwoman but if you could see the curtains you would see that I really am very logical. They're horrible.

Mr. Daldry raises his eyebrows at Dr. Givings.

DR. GIVINGS. And you have tried the usual remedies, rest and relaxation?

MRS. DALDRY.	**MR. DALDRY.**
I do nothing but rest! Nothing but rest!	Yes.

MR. DALDRY. When I met Mrs. Daldry she was seventeen. She was an extraordinary creature. She played the piano. We ate grape jam in the arbor and there I told her I wanted to take care of her and protect her forever, didn't I.

MRS. DALDRY. Yes.

MR. DALDRY. Now I am afraid there is very little sympathy between us.

MRS. DALDRY. I am breaking his heart – . He likes me to be a certain way. Perhaps if I could play the piano again but my fingers will not work.

MR. DALDRY. No, her fingers do not work. In the living room. Or in any other room, if you take my meaning, Dr. Givings.

MRS. DALDRY. Mr. Daldry please do not embarrass me with such vulgarities. I am shocked and disgusted and I will leave the room now.

She leaves the room.
She stands in the living room, flustered.
She sees the electrical lamp and turns it on and off.

DR. GIVINGS. Mr. Daldry, your wife is suffering from hysteria. It is a very clear case. I recommend theraputic electrical massage – weekly – possibly daily, we shall see – sessions. We need to relieve the pressure of her nerves.

You will soon have your blooming wife back, she will regain her color, light and cold will no longer have the same effect on her. You will soon be eating grape jam and wondering how it is that Mrs. Daldry looks so much like a seventeen year old.

MR. DALDRY. Thank you, Dr. Givings. You have no idea what a source of anguish my wife's illness has been to me. And to her, of course.

DR. GIVINGS. Of course. I will have her back for you in an hour's time.

MR. DALDRY. Thank you, Doctor.

Meanwhile, Mrs. Givings has re-entered the living room with the baby.

MRS. DALDRY. *(to Mrs. Givings)*

This lamp is extraordinary.

It hurts my eyes to watch it go on and off

but I enjoy the pain.

It is a kind of religious ecstasy to feel half blind,

do you not think?

MRS. GIVINGS.

Yes, isn't it?

I was not suppposed to meet you

But I'm glad I have.

I hope you find my husband to be a comfort,

I know that I do.

MRS. DALDRY. May I hold your baby?

MRS. GIVINGS. Yes, of course.

DR. GIVINGS. I would ask you to leave Mrs. Daldry here while you take a walk around the grounds. Perhaps it's better if you don't disturb her now, Mr. Daldry.

MR. DALDRY. Of course. Whatever you think best, doctor.

MRS. DALDRY. *(while holding the baby)* What is the baby's name?

MRS. GIVINGS. Letitia. Lotty for short.

Three syllables seemed like too many for a baby.

MRS. DALDRY. Lotty.

During the preceding,
Dr. Givings shakes Mr. Daldry's hand.
Mr. Daldry puts his hat on.
Mr. Daldry gives a brief quizzical glance at the vibrator.
And exits.

ANNIE. *(in the living room, to Mrs. Daldry)* The doctor is ready for you now.

MRS. DALDRY. Oh, no must I go back in there? I would rather hold the baby.

Mr. Daldry enters the living room.

MR. DALDRY. Be a good girl.

Mrs. Daldry hands the baby back to Mrs. Givings.

MRS. DALDRY. Oh, she's beautiful.

MRS. GIVINGS. Isn't she? Too skinny though.

Mrs. Daldry hesitates, looking at the baby.

MR. DALDRY. The doctor is waiting, Sabrina.

MRS. GIVINGS. You'll be just fine.

My husband is a good doctor.
Or so I've been told.
If you'll excuse me, it's time for her nap.

Mrs. Givings exits to the nursery.
Annie leads Mrs. Daldry into the operating theater.
Mr. Daldry surveys the living room and prepares to walk the grounds.
In the operating theater:

DR. GIVINGS. Now then, Mrs. Daldry, I would ask you to remove your clothing but you may keep your underthings on. Please remove your corset, if you would. Annie will place a sheet over your lower regions. We will respect your modesty in every particular.

Mrs. Daldry nods.

DR. GIVINGS. I shall give you privacy.

He turns his back on them, a gentleman, as Mrs. Daldry
undresses with Annie's help.
Mrs. Givings has re-entered the living room
without the baby.
She sees Mr. Daldry.

MRS. GIVINGS. Hello again.

MR. DALDRY. Hello. They are trying to get rid of me. I am supposed to walk about the grounds.

MRS. GIVINGS. But is it not raining, Mr – ?

MR. DALDRY. Daldry.

I don't know.

MRS. GIVINGS. Your name?

MR. DALDRY. No. If it is raining.

MRS. GIVINGS. Then you will have to gamble on whether or not to take an umbrella.

MR. DALDRY. Indeed.

Meanwhile, in the operating theater,

Mrs. Daldry disrobes with Annie's help.
It takes a while to disrobe as she wears a variety of layers.

In the living room, with Mr. Daldry and Mrs. Givings:

MRS. GIVINGS. There are three kinds of people. Those who use umbrellas when it is not raining; those who do not use umbrellas even when it is raining; and those who use umbrellas only and precisely while it rains. Which kind are you, Mr. Daldry?

MR. DALDRY. I use an umbrella while it is raining.

MRS. GIVINGS. That's too bad. I find people who do not use umbrellas while it is raining horribly romantic. Strolling, no *striding*, through the rain, with wet hair, looking at a drop of water on a branch.

MR. DALDRY. My wife is one of those.

MRS. GIVINGS. Oh yes! I could see that.

MR. DALDRY. It's damned annoying. I always worry she'll catch cold.

MRS. DALDRY. You have assisted women in their confinements?

ANNIE. Yes.

MRS. DALDRY. So you have seen every form of torture.

ANNIE. I have seen women in a great deal of pain, yes.

MRS. DALDRY. Hold my hand and I will fall asleep.

ANNIE. Of course.

Annie holds Mrs. Daldry's hand and strokes her hair.
Mrs. Daldry falls asleep.
Throughout the next bit, she drowses, and then wakes and gets dressed with the help of Annie.

In the other room,
Mr. Daldry and Mrs. Givings return from their walk on the grounds.
They are laughing and drenched.
Mrs. Givings shakes out her umbrella.

MRS. GIVINGS. I must be a very inconsistent person! I like to be wet and then I like to be dry and then I like to be wet again!

MR. DALDRY. You are very healthy and robust. I could barely keep up with you.

MRS. GIVINGS. I love to walk – I never had enough exercise as a child so now I walk walk walk no one can keep up with me not even Dr. Givings – that is how he fell in love with me, he said he was determined to keep up with me – he only saw the back of my head before we married because I was always one step ahead. He said he had to marry me to see my face.

Dr. Givings enters.

MRS. GIVINGS. Didn't you darling?

DR. GIVINGS. What's that?

MRS. GIVINGS. Have to marry me in order to see my face?

DR. GIVINGS. I see you have met my wife.

MR. DALDRY. Indeed.

DR. GIVINGS. We had a very successful session. You should find Mrs. Daldry much relaxed.

MR. DALDRY. Excellent.

MRS. GIVINGS. I gave Mr. Daldry a tour of the grounds. We got wet.

DR. GIVINGS. I don't want you catching cold. The baby musn't catch cold at this age.

MRS. GIVINGS. You know I'm healthy as an ox. If only more of my milk would come in. Oh, excuse me, Mr. Daldry that is not polite to mention in mixed company.

MR. DALDRY. Are you advertising for a nurse?

MRS. GIVINGS. Indeed we are.

MR. DALDRY. Our house-keeper recently lost her baby and I believe she still has plentiful milk. Perhaps she could help though we don't want to lose her services, she is very upstanding and all the rest of it, very hard to find, a gem. Self-educated, you see, with the manners of a lady. I don't know if she'd ever take it into her head to be a wet nurse, you know what they say about wet-nurses, nine parts devil, one part cow – but that's what you want, isn't it? A nice young woman who never intended to be a wet nurse but who has milk, milk to spare.

MRS. GIVINGS. Oh, she sounds perfect, we desperately want someone very moral whose child is recently dead.

MRS. GIVINGS.	**DR. GIVINGS.**
Oh, no – what I meant to say is –	What she means to say is –

MRS. GIVINGS. It's only that they say morality goes right through the milk. Mrs. Evans said just the other day, oh I wouldn't use a darkie, the morality goes right through the milk. But in the South, I don't know *what* they do in the South –

MR. DALDRY. Elizabeth our housekeeper is colored but she is very moral, very Christian. She goes to church every week with Mrs. Daldry who is a very devout woman.

MRS. GIVINGS. I see.

DR. GIVINGS. Has she recovered from the death of her child?

MR. DALDRY. As I said, she's a very religious woman resigned to the will of God. And her milk is still plentiful.

MRS. GIVINGS. Darling, I don't know about a – .

DR. GIVINGS. My father was a well-known abolitionist, Mr. Daldry.

MR. DALDRY. I believe I've heard of him. William Givings.

DR. GIVINGS. Yes. *(to Mrs. Givings)* You'd rather have a Negro protestant than an Irish Catholic, wouldn't you?

Mrs. Givings thinks about that.

DR. GIVINGS. Is she married?

MR. DALDRY. Yes.

MRS. GIVINGS. That's good.

MR. DALDRY. To be sure – you don't want an unmarried woman boarding at your house – turn the household upside down – the pretty ones anyway –

He laughs and jostles Dr. Givings. Mrs. Givings stares.
Dr. Givings clears his throat.

MR. DALDRY. That is to say – she's married to a fine man with a steady job.

DR. GIVINGS. We would be happy to take on your house-keeper Elizabeth as a wet nurse. And we can pay handsomely but not so handsomely that she leaves your service. We really are in dire straits because my wife's milk is not adequate, I'm afraid. Bottle-fed babies don't do well in cholera season, they don't do well at all. It's no time to stand on prejudice, Catherine.

MRS. GIVINGS. My husband is a very unconventional man, a scientist. I've no idea what the neighbors will say.

DR. GIVINGS. Let them observe that your baby is growing nice and fat.

Mrs. Daldry enters, looking wonderfully well rested.

MRS. GIVINGS. How well rested you look!

MRS. DALDRY. I feel wonderful. Your husband is a good doctor.

MRS. GIVINGS. Yes he is.

MR. DALDRY. There are roses in your cheeks.

DR. GIVINGS. Is the light bothering you, Mrs. Daldry?

MRS. DALDRY. No, I hardly noticed it. I was horrified when the electric lamp was invented. I so prefer candle-light and I thought, from now on people's faces will look like monsters in the evening, without the help of candle-light. No flicker, no glow. But none of you look like monsters at present, you all look very charming. You are wet, Mr. Daldry.

MR. DALDRY. It is raining, Mrs. Daldry. Shall we?

Mrs. Daldry nods.

MR. DALDRY. Might we borrow an umbrella? I did not anticipate rain.

DR. GIVINGS. To be sure. I always keep an extra umbrella in case of emergencies.

MRS. DALDRY. Thank you, Dr. Givings. I will see you again soon I hope?

DR. GIVINGS. Tomorrow, I believe is best. We will need daily sessions.

MR. DALDRY. Excellent.

Oh – how much do I owe you Doctor? *(in lowered tones, away from the ladies)*

DR. GIVINGS. Not to worry. We'll settle up weekly.

MR. DALDRY. Oh fine, fine.

Then we shall see you tomorrow. And we'll bring Elizabeth with us!

DR. GIVINGS. *(as they exit)* Good-day!

MR. & MRS. DALDRY. Good-day!

MRS. GIVINGS. Good-day!

The door shuts.

MRS. GIVINGS. I'm nervous about bringing a stranger into the house, very nervous indeed.

DR. GIVINGS. Lotty is losing weight, my dear.

MRS. GIVINGS. Yes, of course, it's all my fault.

DR. GIVINGS. I'm not assigning blame, my darling.

MRS. GIVINGS. Whose fault is it then?

DR. GIVINGS. No one's. The body is blameless. Milk is without intention.

MRS. GIVINGS. A good mother has a fat child. And everyone knows it.

DR. GIVINGS. Then it will be a relief to find her a good nurse.

MRS. GIVINGS. Indeed. I cannot wait to meet her.

DR. GIVINGS. Cheer up, my darling. We are healthy and happy, are we not?

MRS. GIVINGS. Yes. *(automatically)*

Yes. *(then, smiling, with sincerity)*

He kisses her on the cheek, and moves to exit.
Mrs. Givings, alone.
End of scene.

Second Scene

Dr. Givings examines Elizabeth in the operating theater.

DR. GIVINGS. It is important to examine you to be sure your milk is healthy.

ELIZABETH. Yes, sir.

DR. GIVINGS. I also need to be sure you haven't any venereal disease that could be passed through the milk to the child. If you could just lie back please…

ELIZABETH. Sir, I'd rather not.

DR. GIVINGS. I'm a man of science, Elizabeth. Believe me, I won't be shocked.

ELIZABETH. Yes, sir.

Sir – you won't touch there, will you?

Mrs. Givings enters the living room.

DR. GIVINGS. I'm going to give you a medical exam, that's all.

She lies back. He covers her with a sheet.
The doorbell rings.
Mrs. Givings answers it.
Mrs. Daldry appears.

MRS. DALDRY. Hello!

MRS. GIVINGS. Hello!

MRS. DALDRY. I was walking the grounds, they're lovely.

MRS. GIVINGS. Why, you look in the bloom of health.

MRS. DALDRY. I played the piano again!

MRS. GIVINGS. What did you play?

MRS. DALDRY. I like to make songs up.

MRS. GIVINGS. Would you play one for me, please oh please?

MRS. DALDRY. I am very shy.

MRS. GIVINGS. No one is shy around me, Mrs. Daldry, I have the most wonderful effect upon shy people, they hear me talk and they think, oh why be shy?

MRS. DALDRY. I don't feel shy around you, Mrs. Givings.

MRS. GIVINGS. I knew it! You see I'm terrible at the piano, I just pick at it with one or two fingers, it's hardly been used, you must play it. The poor thing is *languishing* without a human touch. It is like a piece of dead wood without being played.

MRS. DALDRY. How can I say no?

Mrs. Daldry goes to the piano. She plays a pretty, somber, mysterious little tune.

In the next room:

DR. GIVINGS. Thank you Elizabeth, you were very brave, and you are very healthy. You can get dressed now.

Dr. Givings exits and Elizabeth gets dressed.

MRS. GIVINGS. Oh but that's beautiful! A bit sad, isn't it? Do you think we make sad things into songs in order to hold onto the sadness or to banish it – I think it is to banish the sadness. So then if you write a happy song, is it not sadder than a sad song because by making it you have banished your own happiness into a song? What do you think?

MRS. DALDRY. I don't know.

MRS. GIVINGS. Does it have words?

MRS. DALDRY. No.

MRS. GIVINGS. Oh, but it must have words, Mrs. Daldry, oh it must. I will supply the words, play it again, and I will sing some words with it, how is that?

MRS. DALDRY. All right.

MRS. GIVINGS.

You raise the blinds in the morning
And I like to close them at night.
Together we sleep near the bird house
And forget the electrical light.

Dr. Givings re-enters the operating theater and escorts the now dressed Elizabeth to the living room.

MRS. DALDRY. Well that was very nice.

MRS. GIVINGS. Did you like it? Did it go with your song? Oh I hope you liked it. I hope the song liked the words because the words loved the song!

MRS. DALDRY. The song liked the words.

Dr. Givings enters with Elizabeth.

DR. GIVINGS. Mrs. Givings.

MRS. GIVINGS. Hello darling.

DR. GIVINGS. I have examined Elizabeth and she is very fit and healthy and will be a wonderful nurse to Letitia.

MRS. GIVINGS. Oh, that's marvelous! I'm so sorry about your own child, Elizabeth, that's dreadful.

ELIZABETH. Thank you.

MRS. GIVINGS. What was your child's name or did she have a name yet, oh that would be horrible, I don't know what's worse frankly, a name or no name yet, oh I need to stop talking, when death comes up I just ramble on and on, I'll stop now.

ELIZABETH. His name was Henry Douglas.

MRS. GIVINGS. A boy.

ELIZABETH. Yes.

MRS. GIVINGS. Have you – buried him yet?

ELIZABETH. He's buried at the church-yard, All Soul's. He was baptized before he died and for that I'm grateful.

MRS. GIVINGS. Oh, yes. Baptism, at least, is a comfort – he is in heaven now.

ELIZABETH. I don't like to talk about Henry Douglas. Ma'am.

MRS. GIVINGS. No of course you wouldn't. Forgive me.

MRS. DALDRY. Elizabeth has two other boys. Two lovely boys, very well-behaved.

MRS. GIVINGS. Oh, what a relief. We hope to have extra children, just in case, that is to say, more children. I would love to have a great big brood, all climbing over the furniture, furniture is so dead, that is to say so life-less, I mean so sad, without children.

MRS. DALDRY. I don't have any children.

MRS. GIVINGS. Oh! What a pity.

Mrs. Daldry is visibly agitated.

DR. GIVINGS. Elizabeth, would you like to meet the baby?

ELIZABETH. Yes, sir.

DR. GIVINGS. Catherine, please bring the baby in to Elizabeth. Mrs. Daldry, why don't you come with me.

MRS. DALDRY. Yes, doctor.

Mrs. Givings exit to the nursery.
Elizabeth sits, nervous. She takes off her hat.
Mrs. Daldry and Dr. Givings go to the operating room.

DR. GIVINGS. Did that upset you to talk about children?

MRS. DALDRY. A little.

DR. GIVINGS. Are you feeling nervous?

MRS. DALDRY. My heart is pounding and I feel quite weak.

DR. GIVINGS. Well you just lie down, just lie down, and I will administer treatment.

MRS. DALDRY. Where is Annie today?

DR. GIVINGS. She should be arriving momentarily.

MRS. DALDRY. I do not wish to undress in front of you.

DR. GIVINGS. Yes, of course. I will make some notes. Call out when you are ready for me.

Dr. Givings sits at his desk.
Mrs. Daldry starts to undress.
Mrs. Givings enters with the baby
and gives her to Elizabeth.

MRS. GIVINGS. Well. Here she is!

ELIZABETH. Would you like me to feed her now, ma'am?

MRS. GIVINGS. I suppose. She must be hungry.

Elizabeth sits, holds the baby, undoes her shirt, and begins nursing.
Elizabeth cries, with no sound.
Mrs. Givings watches. Mrs. Givings starts to cry.
Elizabeth notices.

ELIZABETH. Perhaps it would be better if I fed her in the nursery.

MRS. GIVINGS. Yes, I think so.

ELIZABETH. Excuse me.

MRS. GIVINGS. Of course. Just through there.

Elizabeth exits to the nursery with the baby.
Dr. Givings enters the living room.

DR. GIVINGS. Excuse me darling,
What is it?

MRS. GIVINGS. Well, Lotty took to Elizabeth right away. She latched right onto her breast and it made me feel very strange, to see her latched on to another woman's breast. For once it wasn't the baby who was crying. But I feel very queer, I do.

DR. GIVINGS. Now you have to think of the baby and what's best for the baby. She would starve without milk, so think about that and be practical.

MRS. GIVINGS. I don't feel well.

MRS. DALDRY. *(from the operating room)* I'm ready, Dr. Givings.

DR. GIVINGS. I have to attend to Mrs. Daldry. Why don't you have a nice lie-down. Here, I'll shut off the lamp.

He does.

MRS. GIVINGS. I don't want to lie down. I want to feed my own child.

DR. GIVINGS. But you can't, love. Your milk isn't adequate. I love you.

He exits.
She paces around the living room.
She tries to play the song Mrs. Daldry played on the piano in the last scene during the following scene.
She picks at the piano with two fingers.

DR. GIVINGS. Sorry for the delay.

MRS. DALDRY. Not at all.

DR. GIVINGS. Fine weather we're having.

MRS. DALDRY. Mm.

DR. GIVINGS. Chilly but bright.

MRS. DALDRY. Indeed.

DR. GIVINGS. There we are.

> *In the operating room,*
> *Dr. Givings turns on the vibrator.*
> *It makes a loud sound.*
> *Mrs. Givings hears the sound, registers*
> *its oddness, and goes on playing the piano.*
> *Dr. Givings puts the vibrator to Mrs. Daldry's private*
> *parts.*

DR. GIVINGS. This will only take but a few minutes, Mrs. Daldry.

MRS. DALDRY. Oh…

DR. GIVINGS. There there. What are you feeling, Mrs. Daldry?

MRS. DALDRY. It's not working, today it's not working.

> *Dr. Givings adjusts the machine, making it louder.*

DR. GIVINGS. There?

MRS. DALDRY. I don't know.

> *He repositions the machine, under the blankets.*

MRS. DALDRY. Nothing. I feel nothing.

> *He turns it up again. The vibrating noise stops all*
> *together. And all the lights go out.*

DR. GIVINGS. Oh, dear.

MRS. DALDRY. Did I make it stop?

DR. GIVINGS. It's not your fault. Electrical failure.

> *Mrs. Givings looks up*
> *in the dark of the living room.*
> *She lights several candles.*
> *Annie enters the operating room.*

DR. GIVINGS. Well, I'm glad you're here, Annie, we've had a power failure.

MRS. DALDRY. My head.

ANNIE. Oh, dear Mrs. Daldry, are you ill?

DR. GIVINGS. *(to Annie, in low tones)* I have been trying these last three minutes, it's never taken longer than three minutes with this machine.

ANNIE. Should I try the manual treatment, Dr. Givings?

DR. GIVINGS. Yes, why don't you, I will go look into this. Good-day Mrs. Daldry, Annie.

MRS. DALDRY. What is the manual treatment?

ANNIE. You just lie back.

> *In the near dark,*
> *Annie puts her hand under the sheet and begins to stim-*
> *ulate Mrs. Daldry. We certainly do not see this, and the*
> *actress needn't simulate it exactly, but under the sheets,*
> *Mrs. Daldry has a female ejaculation.*

MRS. DALDRY. Oh! Everything is quite wet! I don't know what's happened,

I'm sorry – I. How embarrassing.

ANNIE. That happens from time to time, Mrs. Daldry, I'll change the sheets.

Aristotle talked all about it.

MRS. DALDRY. Aristotle?

ANNIE. Yes.

MRS. DALDRY. Do you read Greek?

ANNIE. Yes.

MRS. DALDRY. My goodness.

ANNIE. I'm going to wash my hands.

MRS. DALDRY. Of course.

> *Meanwhile, in the other room, Elizabeth enters.*
> *The living room is now lit with several candles.*

ELIZABETH. Do you need me this evening, Mrs. Givings?

MRS. GIVINGS. Perhaps after supper?

ELIZABETH. All right.

> *Elizabeth turns to go.*

MRS. GIVINGS. Wait a moment.

Elizabeth, when the milk comes in, can you feel any love for the child?

ELIZABETH. I try not to think of love. I try not to think of Henry Douglas.

MRS. GIVINGS. Of course. Do you want more children, Elizabeth? That is a tactless question, you don't need to answer, forgive me, sometimes I say whatever is in my head. I want more children and my husband desperately wants more children but I am afraid of another birth, aren't you? When I gave birth I remember so clearly, the moment her head was coming out of my body, I thought: Why would any rational creature do this twice, knowing what I know now? And then she came out and clambered right onto my breast and tried to eat me, she was so hungry, so hungry it terrified me – her hunger. And I thought: is that the first emotion? Hunger? And not hunger for *food* but wanting to eat other *people*? Specifically one's mother? And then I thought – isn't it strange, isn't it strange about Jesus? That is to say, about Jesus being a man? For it is women who are eaten – who turn their bodies into food – I gave up my blood – there was so much blood – and I gave up my body – but I couldn't feed her, could not turn my body into food, and she was *so hungry*. I suppose that makes me an inferior kind of woman and a very inferior kind of Jesus.

ELIZABETH. Hmm.

MRS. GIVINGS. Oh, dear, they said you were very religious, that must have sounded –

ELIZABETH. I *was* very religious.

MRS. GIVINGS. Oh – I'm sorry, I –

ELIZABETH. I thought of Jesus while I was giving birth, like you. But I wasn't thinking about why was He a man. I was thinking, please save me Jesus. And He did. Now why He didn't save my Henry I don't know, so I stopped believing in Him.

MRS. GIVINGS. Oh!

The light comes back on.

Ah, the electricity is back.

Mrs. Daldry enters, dressed.

MRS. DALDRY. Hello.

MRS. GIVINGS. Hello!

ELIZABETH. Hello.

MRS. GIVINGS. You look refreshed.

MRS. DALDRY. Do I?

MRS. GIVINGS. Oh, yes. Would you play us something on the piano, I am sure Elizabeth would love to hear you play.

ELIZABETH. I have to get back to my boys for supper.

MRS. GIVINGS. Oh stay for just one song.

MRS. DALDRY. All right.

Mrs. Daldry plays a little tune. It is sad.
They all listen to the song.
Elizabeth cries but no one sees her crying.
Annie enters.

ANNIE. What a pretty song, Mrs. Daldry.

MRS. DALDRY. Thank you, Annie.

ELIZABETH. I must go.

MRS. DALDRY. And I.

ANNIE. I am walking in your direction.

MRS. GIVINGS. Good-bye then, everyone gets a good walk except for me. Come again tomorrow or I will be very dull.

Elizabeth lingers.

MRS. GIVINGS. What is it, Elizabeth?

ELIZABETH. Do you pay me now, or later?

MRS. GIVINGS. Oh goodness! I haven't any money, I'll have to ask my husband. Perhaps we can settle up weekly?

ELIZABETH. That's fine. Good-bye.

MRS. GIVINGS. Good-bye.

They all exit.
Mrs. Givings blows the candles out.
Dr. Givings enters, pleased that the power is back on.

DR. GIVINGS. The power is back on! One day whole cities will be electrified. Mr. Edison is the man to do it.

MRS. GIVINGS. Don't talk to me about electricity.

You know how it bores me.

Everyone is gone.

And we are alone.

DR. GIVINGS. Indeed we are.

MRS. GIVINGS. I shall turn this off.

She kisses him.

DR. GIVINGS. Shall we go upstairs?

MRS. GIVINGS. Or stay here…

DR. GIVINGS. In the living room?

MRS. GIVINGS. I suppose it is for living in.

They move to the sofa, awkward.
They kiss again, with polite desire.
The doorbell rings.
They look at each other as though to say:
Don't answer that.

DR. GIVINGS. I'll get it.

Dr. Givings turns on the light and opens the door.

Mrs. Givings blinks.

DR. GIVINGS. Mrs. Daldry?

MRS. DALDRY. I forgot my hat.

DR. GIVINGS. You look flushed. Are you all right?

MRS. DALDRY. Perhaps the walk over-excited me. I am not used to walking that much in one day. Annie and I were walking rather quickly, and discussing – well – she knows Greek, can you imagine – I feel faint.

Mrs. Daldry half-collapses on the arm of a chair.
Dr. Givings goes to her.

MRS. GIVINGS. Oh!

DR. GIVINGS. There, there Mrs. Daldry. Why don't you come see me in the operating theater. The electricity is back on.

MRS. DALDRY. Perhaps I'm intruding on your domestic life.

DR. GIVINGS. Not at all.

MRS. GIVINGS. Not at all.

DR. GIVINGS. This way. Mrs. Givings, why don't you go to the nursery.

MRS. GIVINGS. Yes, dear.

Dr. Givings and Mrs. Daldry go into the operating room. Mrs. Givings listens at the door.

DR. GIVINGS. No need to undress all the way, as you're not feeling well, just lie down gently. Are you still feeling faint?

MRS. DALDRY. A little.

She shakes her head, taking her gloves off.

DR. GIVINGS. Are you often subject to faintness?

MRS. DALDRY. No more than once a week, I daresay.

DR. GIVINGS. I see. We'll set you to rights, no worries. Are you ready?

She nods.
He puts the vibrator down her bloomers.
Mrs. Givings listens at the door.

MRS. DALDRY. Oh. Oh. No.

Mrs. Givings cocks her head.

DR. GIVINGS. Tell me what you're feeling.

MRS. DALDRY. I don't – want – a machine.

DR. GIVINGS. Any fluid, Mrs. Daldry?

MRS. DALDRY. No. Nothing.

DR. GIVINGS. I will try using a finger as well as the instrument to replicate Annie's experiment. Vulvular massage has been discounted in many circles but occasionally with the proper diagnosis and method it is just the thing.

He puts a finger under the sheets, and continues with the vibrator.

MRS. DALDRY. Oh, oh, oh!

DR. GIVINGS. There, there, Mrs. Daldry, let it all out.

MRS. DALDRY. Oh, Annie!

DR. GIVINGS. Excuse me?

MRS. DALDRY. Please leave me. I feel much relieved.

DR. GIVINGS. I will wash up and let you get sorted. Take your time.

Mrs. Givings knocks at the door of the operating theater.

DR. GIVINGS. Excuse me. *(to Mrs. Daldry)*

He exits to the living room.

What is it? The baby? *(to Mrs. Givings)*

MRS. GIVINGS. What is that sound? What were you doing?

DR. GIVINGS. Electrical therapy, my dear. Very successful session.

MRS. GIVINGS. I wish to see it.

DR. GIVINGS. You would not understand. Leave me my dry boring science and I will give you the rest of the world. You said yourself that my electricity bored you.

MRS. GIVINGS. I insist on seeing your machine now.

DR. GIVINGS. Are you going to force me to lock my laboratory?

MRS. GIVINGS. I am your wife.

DR. GIVINGS. And happily you are my blooming young wife without a hint of neurosis and in no need of my inventions or experiments.

MRS. GIVINGS. Experiment on me!

DR. GIVINGS. I can assure you that you would not like it.

MRS. GIVINGS. Experiment on me!

DR. GIVINGS. It would be unseemly for a man of science to do experiments on his wife. I'd lose my credibility. Now would you have the good grace to be quiet while Mrs. Daldry is in the next room –

Mrs. Daldry enters the living room, looking the very picture of health.

MRS. DALDRY. Do not let me forget my hat again.

MRS. GIVINGS. It is right here.

MRS. DALDRY. Ah.

Thank you Dr. Givings.

Mrs. Givings hands Mrs. Daldry her hat.

DR. GIVINGS. Not at all. Good-bye.

MRS. DALDRY. Good-bye.

MRS. GIVINGS. Good-bye.

DR. GIVINGS. I'm going to the club. Mr. Edison's man is electrocuting dogs this evening. He is out to prove the deadliness of the alternating current over and above direct current. I think it's hogwash. In alternating current, the current flips back and forth, back and – you see how much this bores you.

He locks the door of the operating theater and puts the key in his pocket.

MRS. GIVINGS. Yes it is very boring good-bye and don't kiss me good-bye please.

DR. GIVINGS. Very well.

He leaves.
She storms.
She goes towards the operating theater.
She jiggles the door.
The doorbell rings.

MRS. DALDRY. I've forgotten my gloves, I'm so sorry, what must you think of me.

MRS. GIVINGS. Oh, I'm so happy to see you! My husband has just gone to the club and I am bored out of my mind.

MRS. DALDRY. I think my gloves are in the other room.

MRS. GIVINGS. It is locked.

MRS. DALDRY. Oh, I can come back tomorrow for my gloves.

MRS. GIVINGS. No, please stay. I have developed the most insatiable curiosity about my husband's operating theater. Perhaps you can tell me how it works.

MRS. DALDRY. Oh – no – I don't know how it works –

MRS. GIVINGS. He plugs it in, he turns it on, and then?

MRS. DALDRY. He applies electrical current to my – to my body – to release the magnetic fluid. That is what he says. Because there is excess fluid in my womb, causing my hysterical symptoms.

MRS. GIVINGS. Fluid?

MRS. DALDRY. Yes.

Really, I must go now –

MRS. GIVINGS. You sounded like this: oh, oh, ah-ee!

MRS. DALDRY. You were listening?

MRS. GIVINGS. It was loud.

MRS. DALDRY. Oh, dear. I will leave you now.

MRS. GIVINGS. Stay for tea.

Where does my husband place the electrical device?

MRS. DALDRY. *(pointing vaguely to her knees)* Just here.

MRS. GIVINGS. Hm.

And does it give you a pleasurable or a painful sensation?

MRS. DALDRY. Pleasure, and pain all at once – electrical current runs through my entire body – I see light – patterns of light, under my eye-lids – and a kind of white-hot coal on my feet – and I shudder violently, as though struck by a terrible lightning – and then a darkness descends, and I want to sleep.

MRS. GIVINGS. I never heard of anything so strange.

MRS. DALDRY. Let's talk of other things. They electrocuted an elephant at Coney Island.

MRS. GIVINGS. Yes, I've heard.

MRS. DALDRY. It is getting dark.

MRS. GIVINGS. I will turn the lamp on.

MRS. DALDRY. Please, don't.

They sit in the dark.

MRS. DALDRY. Can you imagine a time when all will be electric, all will be plugged in, why it will not stop at lights, but the way we cook our eggs and the way we get our chickens to lay their eggs too. Mr. Edison invented a recording device which he says will change everything, *it will record the last wishes of the dying.* Can you imagine? A man may know the voice of his great great grandfather, may know his last wishes. And what will become of the human body? Electrical arms perhaps. Even the fireflies will become electric.

MRS. GIVINGS. Electrical fireflies.

MRS. DALDRY. Yes.

MRS. GIVINGS. Electrical pianos.

MRS. DALDRY. God forbid.

MRS. GIVINGS. Oh, to think of never carrying a candle! Not to walk through a hallway at night, holding a candle, afraid of tripping in the dark, starting a fire, it makes one more solemn, do you not think? Or to blow out a candle – how beautiful! With one's own breath, to extinguish the light! Do you think our children's children will be less solemn? A flick of the finger – and all is lit! A flick of the finger, and all is dark! On, off, on off! We could change our minds a dozen times a second! On, off, on off! We shall be like gods!

MRS. DALDRY. I'm afraid so.

MRS. GIVINGS. Have you a hat pin?

MRS. DALDRY. Yes.

She hands Mrs. Givings a pin from her hat.
Mrs. Givings goes to pick the lock of the operating theater.

MRS. GIVINGS. I will just retrieve your gloves.

Mrs. Givings enters the operating theater.
Mrs. Daldry is on her heels.
Mrs. Givings looks around.

MRS. GIVINGS. Is this it?

MRS. DALDRY. Yes.

MRS. GIVINGS. How extraordinary. It looks like a farming tool.

Where do you put it?

MRS. DALDRY. Here.

Mrs. Givings puts the vibrator to her private parts, over her skirt.

MRS. GIVINGS. I see.

Where's the switch?

MRS. DALDRY. I've no idea.

Mrs. Givings finds the switch.
The vibrator turns on.

MRS. GIVINGS. What a sound!

MRS. DALDRY. I will hold it in place for you.

She does.

MRS. GIVINGS. Is it heavy?

MRS. DALDRY. Tolerably.

MRS. GIVINGS. Well I don't see what all the fuss is about.

MRS. DALDRY. Sometimes I close my eyes.

Mrs. Givings closes her eyes.
Mrs. Daldry gently puts the vibrator
under Mrs. Givings' skirt.
The buzz of the vibrator,
for longer than is comfortable.

MRS. GIVINGS. Oh!

Oh!

Mrs. Givings climaxes.
And as she does so, she weeps.

MRS. GIVINGS. Well that was very awful – it was a very dreadful strange feeling, I see why he has been keeping it from me.

MRS. DALDRY. Yes.

MRS. GIVINGS. Would you like a go – ?

MRS. DALDRY. Oh, no only the doctor can administer the treatment.

MRS. GIVINGS. I don't see why. It looks quite simple. In this day and age, all one has to know how to do is press a button or pull a switch. I'll hold it for you.

MRS. DALDRY. All right. Wait – *(she listens)*
Is that not your husband's carriage?

MRS. GIVINGS. I can't hear a thing.

MRS. DALDRY. I hear horse's hooves.

MRS. GIVINGS. You're imagining things. He won't be home from the club until at least 7 o'clock.

MRS. DALDRY. Are you sure?

MRS. GIVINGS. Oh yes, when he starts talking about electricity he cannot stop.

MRS. DALDRY. Well then.

MRS. GIVINGS. Are you ready?

MRS. DALDRY. I think so.

MRS. GIVINGS. Here we go!

Mrs. Givings puts the vibrator to
Mrs. Daldry's private parts.
They look heavenwards.
The steady hum of the vibrator. Transcendent music.
A curtain falls.
The end of the act.

Act II

First Scene

Two weeks or so later.
Dr. Givings and Leo,
in the operating theater.

LEO. And then she left, very abruptly, for Italy.

DR. GIVINGS. I see.

LEO. It was a terrible shock.

I had been studying in Florence for the year. They are exacting masters over there – the line must be just so – the proportion just so – there is no freedom – you sharpen your pencil with a knife, as Leonardo sharpened his pencil. It was heaven. Not to have freedom. No freedom in art, but in life, life! The peaches there tasted like peaches, the rain like rain. I met the woman in question in Florence. A very beautiful woman. (I know. No one ever said: I fell in love with a woman in Italy – a very ugly woman.) But she *was* beautiful. Perhaps not classically, but nevermind…We met at the Uffizi. She was looking at the sculptures with no embarassment, no embarassment at all. I painted her face all summer. When she kissed she kissed with her whole body, not like American women who kiss only with their lips.

DR. GIVINGS. Mm.

LEO. You are perhaps shocked, doctor, that I kissed her before marriage. I am a devotee of nature and I wished to avoid the fate of my boyhood friend. On his wedding night he was repulsed by his wife's body. He said, when she disrobed for the first time, he saw something

LEO. *(cont.)* monstrous. What, what? I asked. She had body hair, he said, down there! Like a beast! You see, he had seen the female form only in marble statues – no body hair! You are a scientist, that must amuse you.

DR. GIVINGS. What men do not observe because their intellect prevents them from seeing would fill many books.

LEO. Indeed.

DR. GIVINGS. What happened to your friend?

LEO. He is now a very famous art critic. His marriage went unconsummated for three years and was then anulled. I did not wish such a fate for myself, and so, while lips were willing and free and soft, I kissed them. Oh yes, I kissed them.

She did not come from a good family and her English was not very good but I did not care. Her soul lept out of her eyes. When I painted her I felt I could paint souls. Her soul hovered, just here, and I could see it. *(He gestures to a place about two inches from the eyes.)* So when I painted I painted two inches away from the eyes, not the eyes themselves – it was a revelation! – I digress.

Mrs. Givings enters the other room and arranges tea things.

LEO. She journeyed with me to England to meet my parents, to announce the engagement. And then, the following morning, she fled. Back to Italy! No word, no letter! No answer to my inquiries! Nothing! And my whole body revolted against me. Headaches, eyesight, weakness, nausea…

DR. GIVINGS. And this weakness has persisted, for, what – ?

LEO. Nine months.

DR. GIVINGS. In your extremities?

LEO. Yes. But the weakness in my eyes is perhaps the worst, because of my inability to paint.

DR. GIVINGS. So you haven't painted for nine months?

LEO. You can't paint in the dark.

DR. GIVINGS. It is very rare, a case of hysteria in a man, but of course we do see it.

LEO. Is it treatable?

DR. GIVINGS. I believe it is. I'd like you to undress to your underthings and lie down on the table. Annie, my assistant, will be in shortly.

Elizabeth enters the living room with the baby.

LEO. I did not know there would be a lady in attendance.

DR. GIVINGS. She is the soul of tact and reserve.

Leo undresses.
Meanwhile, in the living room:

MRS. GIVINGS. *(to Elizabeth)* Was she a good eater?

ELIZABETH. An angel.

MRS. GIVINGS. Thank you, Elizabeth.

ELIZABETH. I think that babies are angels when they drink only milk, that first year. They could fly right back to where they came from, to the milk in the clouds. When they get teeth it is the beginning of the end, they become animals and there's no going back.

MRS. GIVINGS. Yes.

ELIZABETH. But this one's still an angel, no teeth.

Elizabeth touches the baby's cheek.
The baby smiles.
Mrs. Givings is jealous.

MRS. GIVINGS. Well.

That will be all now, Elizabeth.

ELIZABETH. I'll just get my things.

Elizabeth exits to the nursery.
Leo is now undressed.
Dr. Givings enters the operating theater.
Mrs. Givings is holding the baby.
Annie has draped a sheet over Leo.
Mrs. Givings alone with the baby.

MRS. GIVINGS. No smile?

You were smiling for Elizabeth.

(singing quietly)

You raise the blinds in the morning

And I like to close them at night

Together we sleep near the birdhouse

And forget the electrical light.

In the operating theater:

DR. GIVINGS. This, Leo, is what I call the Chattanooga vibrator. My own invention. It slips into the anal cavity.

LEO. Indeed.

DR. GIVINGS. Just face that direction, and curl up a bit, hugging your knees into your chest.

Annie will just operate the foot pedal which controls the speed.

It functions – much like a sewing machine.

LEO. Ah.

Dr. Givings plugs the vibrator in.

DR. GIVINGS. We are going to stimulate the prostate gland. Are you ready?

LEO. I think so.

He puts the vibrator down Leo's underthings.
Annie assists.
Leo looks troubled.
Leo looks shocked.
Leo has an anal paroxysm.

LEO. Oh.

Oh!

Oh.

Mrs. Givings goes to the door – a man's voice?

DR. GIVINGS. Excellent! I think we can stop now for the day.

How are you feeling?

Would you like a cup of tea?

LEO. I would love a cup of tea.

Dr. Givings enters the living room.

MRS. GIVINGS. Hello, darling. How is *work?*

DR. GIVINGS. A new patient. An interesting case. Very rare.

MRS. GIVINGS. A man?

DR. GIVINGS. How did you know?

MRS. GIVINGS. I heard a man's voice.

DR. GIVINGS. I did not know the door was quite so porous.

MRS. GIVINGS. But why would a man come to see you?

DR. GIVINGS. Hysteria is very rare in a man, but then again, he is an artist.

Perhaps you should take the baby for a walk, so that you don't chance running into him.

MRS. GIVINGS. I believe the baby is still hungry – I'll just go and find Elizabeth.

DR. GIVINGS. Yes.

She exits with the baby. Dr. Givings gets tea.
Meanwhile Leo has gotten dressed with Annie's assistance.

LEO. Thank you.

How odd.

Dr. Givings enters and hands Leo tea.

LEO. Lovely.

DR. GIVINGS. I'll see you tomorrow. I believe daily sessions will be best at this early stage.

Feel free to use the grounds.

LEO. Excellent. Thank you, Doctor.

DR. GIVINGS. Of course. See you tomorrow then.

LEO. Yes, yes, of course.

Leo enters the living room at the exact moment that Mrs. Givings enters without the baby.

MRS. GIVINGS. Hello.

LEO. Hello.

MRS. GIVINGS. Mrs. Givings.

LEO. You are the doctor's wife?

MRS. GIVINGS. I am. He seldom has men here. What a rare treat to make your acquaintance!

She looks at him, puzzled, remembering her own experience with the vibrator and wondering how on earth it is used on men.

LEO. Leonard Irving.

MRS. GIVINGS. Pleased to meet you, Mr. Irving.

LEO. And you.

He kisses her hand.

MRS. GIVINGS. So old fashioned.

LEO. I'm afraid everyone goes around these days saying: I am a modern man, I am a modern woman, it's the modern age, after all. But I detest modernity.

MRS. GIVINGS. Do you! How contrary. Are you a very contrary person?

LEO. Some might say so.

MRS. GIVINGS. The cut of your coat is very old fashioned.

LEO. It's my father's old coat. I can't be bothered with the cut of a coat. I throw on whatever my father leaves for rags.

Leo looks at the lamp and squints.

MRS. GIVINGS. Is the lamp too much for your eyes?

LEO. The light has troubled me greatly for the past nine months, but I feel better presently.

She shuts the lamp off.

MRS. GIVINGS. Just in case.

LEO. When Edison's light came out, they were all saying, my God! – light like the sunset of an Italian autumn… no smoke, no odor, a light without flame, without danger!* But to me, Mrs. Givings, a light without flame isn't divine – a light without flame – is like –

MRS. GIVINGS. What?

LEO. I cannot say.

MRS. GIVINGS. Why not?

LEO. I hardly know you. I would offend your feminine sensibilities.

MRS. GIVINGS. Oh, no need to be shy around me, I just blurt anything out.

LEO. Well, then light without flame is like having relations with a prostitute. No flame of love or desire, only the outer trappings of – the act. And without love – without the mental quickening – the eyes – the blood – without the heart – or intellect – bodies are meat. Meat and bone and levers and technicalities.

MRS. GIVINGS. Well perhaps you were right. Perhaps you ought not to have said.

LEO. Not that I've ever known any prostitutes – intimately –

MRS. GIVINGS. *(overlapping with intimately)* I wasn't implying –

LEO. It's only a metaphor –

MRS. GIVINGS. Of course.

It is awkward.
They sit there, in the gathering darkness.

LEO. I love this time of afternoon, when the world is becoming dark, and you can see outside your window – lights in the neighboring windows coming on. One yellow – one almost white – little squares of light, other people's lives – sheltered against the night, so hopeful. Ridiculous, isn't it, to have so much hope, to think a little square of light could blot out the darkness – and yet – another comes on – and see –

He brings her to the window and shows her.

MRS. GIVINGS. Yes – one – then two –

LEO. Look – there – another window lit – golden – the rest of the house dark – an incomplete painting. I love incomplete paintings – why do painters always *insist* upon finishing paintings? It's unaccountable – *life is not like that!*

MRS. GIVINGS. Oh!

LEO. And the ones *Michelangelo* never finished – do you know them? – ghosts of lines hovering in the background. Have you ever seen *Virgin and Child with the Angels?*

MRS. GIVINGS. I have never been to Italy.

LEO. Oh you must go, and upon arrival, you must go directly to see that painting – the incomplete lines of God – they cannot be filled in because they would be too beautiful, they would shock the senses, and so they are *almost there* – women or angels – exchanging confidences – coming into being. A woman who is two-thirds done is nearer to God. A young woman on the verge of knowing herself is the most attractive thing on this earth to a man for this very reason.

MRS. GIVINGS. Do you think so?

LEO. Oh, yes.

They sit for a moment in the dark.
Mrs. Givings suppresses her usual desire to speak
because sitting next to Leo is an entirely new category of
being for her.
The door-bell rings.

MRS. GIVINGS. Excuse me.

Mrs. Givings jumps
and answers the door.
It is Mrs. Daldry.

MRS. GIVINGS. Mrs. Daldry!

MRS. DALDRY. Hello. Am I early? I think that I am early.

MRS. GIVINGS. I have just made the acquaintance of Mr. Irving.

MRS. DALDRY. Pleased to meet you.

But you are in the dark.

Mrs. Givings switches on the lamp.
Leo is riveted by Mrs. Daldry's fragile beauty.
After his unexpected paroxysm, he would fall in love
with whatever creature crossed his path.

LEO. I must go. A thousand paintings. That is to say – a thousand apologies, as it were, for my rudeness at leaving so suddenly, I now have a thousand paintings to make. A bolt from the blue! I must order a new canvas. Several. Immediately. Good-bye.

He runs.

MRS. GIVINGS. What an interesting young man.

MRS. DALDRY. Yes.

MRS. GIVINGS. A painter.

MRS. DALDRY. Indeed!

Mrs. Givings makes sure they are alone.

MRS. GIVINGS. Mrs. Daldry, I have been wanting to speak to you ever since our adventure with the hat-pin. You told me that you saw light when my husband treats you, and then you got drowsy and wanted to sleep. Well, I had such different sensations I wonder if it can be the same instrument at all. I was not the least bit drowsy afterwards. In fact, I was overcome by the desire to walk, or run, or climb a tree! How could one device cause such opposite reactions. Perhaps it is because I am well and you are ill.

MRS. DALDRY. I do not know. I have been so worried that your husband might find out and get upset with us and suspend the treatment.

MRS. GIVINGS. I do not care. I am determined to use the device again and unlock the mystery as to why it makes you drowsy and makes me very excitable. Why, I feel like a scientist!

Dr. Givings enters.

DR. GIVINGS. Ah, Mrs. Daldry, Catherine. We are ready for you in the next room.

MRS. DALDRY. Yes.

Dr. Givings shoots a look at Mrs. Givings for speaking with his patient.
He guides Mrs. Daldry to the operating theater.

DR. GIVINGS. Right this way.

Looking well, looking well. Your appetite has improved, no?

MRS. DALDRY. I daresay it has.

DR. GIVINGS. Wonderful!

They go into the operating theater.
Mrs. Givings watches them go.
The doorbell rings.
Mrs. Givings answers it.

LEO. I'm sorry, I forgot my scarf.

I left in such a state.

MRS. GIVINGS. I am very glad you have returned, Mr. Irving. I am all by myself as Mrs. Daldry has gone in to get electrical therapy and I, the wife, am left to my own *devices.* As it were.

LEO. I'm not sure what you mean, Mrs. Givings.

MRS. GIVINGS. Have some more tea.

She pours.

LEO. I don't want to impose.

MRS. GIVINGS. You'll have to wait for them to finish before you can retrieve your scarf. Sit.

MRS. GIVINGS. Sugar?

LEO. No thank you. Sugar is for women and small, fat boys. Lovely.

Dr. Givings plugs in the vibrator while Mrs. Daldry gets undressed.
The sound of the vibrator. They talk over it.

MRS. GIVINGS. It's fine whether we're having for November.

LEO. Yes. Though dark.

MRS. GIVINGS. Yes, it is dark.

Mrs. Daldry moans from the other room.
Leo speaks more loudly.

LEO. Dark so early. Dark and the trees so tall and naked. I think November is the tallest month because when the trees have lost their leaves they look so much taller. Tall in a – lonely way.

Mrs. Daldry moans.

LEO. Yes – November is a tall month – October is a round month – April is a – skinny month –

MRS. GIVINGS. Oh do stop talking of the seasons!

LEO. Excuse me?

MRS. GIVINGS. We talk, we talk, and we surround ourselves with plants, with teapots, with little statuettes to give ourselves a feeling of home, of permenancy, as if with enough heavy objects, perhaps the world won't shatter into a million pieces, perhaps the house will not fly away, but I experienced something the other day, Mr. Irving, something to shatter a statuette, to shatter an elephant. Here is my riddle: what is a thing that can put a man to death and also bring him back to life again. Will you answer?

LEO. That is easy.

MRS. GIVINGS. Is it?

LEO. Love.

MRS. GIVINGS. No. Electricity.

Meanwhile, Mrs. Daldry has a loud paroxysm in the next room.

DR. GIVINGS. Very good, Mrs. Daldry.

Leo and Mrs. Givings look at each other.
Elizabeth enters with her coat.

ELIZABETH. She ate again and now she's sleeping. I never had a girl. When she eats, she eats so quietly, so politely, not like my boys, who were ravenous.

MRS. GIVINGS. Why thank you Elizabeth.

LEO. You are the baby's nurse?

ELIZABETH. *(to Leo)* Oh, excuse me, I did not see you – I would not have spoken of – Yes, I am the baby's nurse.

LEO. I should like to paint you nursing the baby.

ELIZABETH. That would not be –

LEO. A Madonna for our times. A Madonna after the Civil War –

ELIZABETH. Sir.

LEO. Oh dear, have I displeased you?

MRS. GIVINGS. You'll have to excuse us, Elizabeth, the men in my household are very unorthodox, artists and scientists don't care at all about convention, do they?

LEO. Since your husband has been treating me, I feel full of the most wild creative energies. I could paint all night, and everyone seems full of beauty. You, Elizabeth, are beautiful and you ought to be in a painting.

ELIZABETH. I've never had a man in the room when I've nursed a baby. My husband of course has seen me nurse my own but that is different.

LEO. I would pay you handsomely. And during your regular work hours, just triple the salary, and pretend I am not there while you work.

ELIZABETH. Triple the salary?

LEO. Yes. I cannot imagine she pays you very much for your services.

MRS. GIVINGS. Mr. Irving, really –

LEO. I will pay you ten dollars an hour for your services.

Elizabeth and Mrs. Givings look at each other, shocked. (Ten dollars was the equivalent of one hundred and seventy-five dollars or so.)

ELIZABETH. I will sit for you. But do not tell my husband and please disguise my features. And so that nothing would seem improper, I would like Mrs. Givings to sit in the room with us.

LEO. You must have a beautiful dress to wear, or a robe. Have you a dressing gown we could borrow?

MRS. GIVINGS. I –

LEO. It must be something that will allow the breast out, so that she may give suck.

Mrs. Givings is shocked.
Mrs. Daldry and Dr. Givings enter.

DR. GIVINGS. Hello, Leo. I do not like that my patients should be scheduled so that they meet up – I'm so sorry –

LEO. I left my scarf.

DR. GIVINGS. Ah, go right ahead and get it, we are finished.

MRS. DALDRY. *(sensually, to Leo)* Hello.

LEO. Hello.

The doorbell rings. It is Mr. Daldry.

DR. GIVINGS. Hello, Mr. Daldry.

MR. DALDRY. Doctor.

LEO. I will just fetch my scarf.

In the other room Leo looks at the vibrating machine. He wonders how it might be used on a woman.

MR. DALDRY. You are looking well, Mrs. Daldry. You looked well this morning but you have even more color in your cheeks now.

DR. GIVINGS. Isn't the improvement amazing?

MR. DALDRY. Indeed! I think she might be ready to stop treatments.

MRS. DALDRY. I think that would be premature. I am not cured yet.

MR. DALDRY. But much improved.

DR. GIVINGS. Yes.

MR. DALDRY. You are a magician, doctor.

Leo enters.

LEO. I'd forgotten my scarf.

DR. GIVINGS. Leo Irving.

MR. DALDRY. Dick Daldry.

LEO. Pleased to meet you.

MR. DALDRY. I am glad you found your scarf. It's snowing.

MRS. GIVINGS. Oh! Is it?

MRS. DALDRY. In November?

MR. DALDRY. Indeed. I brought your mackintosh, my dear.

MRS. DALDRY. Thank you.

MR. DALDRY. Thank you, doctor.

DR. GIVINGS. Not at all.

LEO. I will follow you out, we can all walk together.

Mrs. Daldry, Mr. Daldry, Elizabeth, and Leo leave.

DR. GIVINGS. Good-bye.

MRS. DALDRY. Good-bye.

MR. DALDRY. Good-bye.

ELIZABETH. Good-bye.

LEO. Good-bye.

MRS. GIVINGS. Good-bye!

Dr. Givings shuts the door.

DR. GIVINGS. What is it?

MRS. GIVINGS. I think we ought to let Elizabeth go.

DR. GIVINGS. Whatever for?

Letitia is blooming and rosy and positively fat.

MRS. GIVINGS. I think Elizabeth is becoming attached to the baby.

DR. GIVINGS. You want her to give love to the baby but not too much love.

MRS. GIVINGS. Precisely.

DR. GIVINGS. I shall never understand women.

MRS. GIVINGS. I am still leaking bits of gray milk. It is as though my body is crying.

DR. GIVINGS. Oh, darling. You'll be back to normal in no time. And it's good for you to give up nursing, we can have another child more quickly.

MRS. GIVINGS. Another child! I can hardly – !

She won't even look at me!

DR. GIVINGS. Who?

MRS. GIVINGS. The baby!

She won't smile at me!

I am not a good mother. I do nothing! I pour the tea!

I wish you to use your machine on me.

DR. GIVINGS. Darling, it's for women who are ill. It would probably have no effect on you at all, as you're perfectly healthy.

MRS. GIVINGS. I am not healthy. I feel restless, and excitable, and I cry at the smallest thing. You help countless other women but me, your wife, you pat on the head.

DR. GIVINGS. What is the matter?

MRS. GIVINGS. She knows where to get comfort and love, and it is not from me.

DR. GIVINGS. You are her mother!

MRS. GIVINGS. In name only.

Milk is comfort, milk is love.

How will she learn to love me?

DR. GIVINGS. You do seem to be suffering, perhaps from the excess fluid of milk. I can perhaps try the treatment on you although it makes me nervous. But don't go round telling your friends. It must not get out in the scientific community that I am treating my own wife.

MRS. GIVINGS. Now?

DR. GIVINGS. I haven't any other patients for an hour.

MRS. GIVINGS. Now that you've given way I feel quite frightened.

DR. GIVINGS. There's nothing to be frightened of, darling, come along, I'll show you.

He leads her to the operating theater.

DR. GIVINGS. First you undress to your under-things. I shall turn around.

MRS. GIVINGS. Do all the women undress to their under-things?

DR. GIVINGS. It's medicine, my love.

She starts to undress and realizes there are too many buttons in the back.

MRS. GIVINGS. I can't do this bit without your help.

DR. GIVINGS. Oh – sorry.

He helps her with the buttons and then turns round again, a gentleman.

DR. GIVINGS. Is that all right?

MRS. GIVINGS. Yes.

She finishes undressing herself.
He plugs in the vibrator.

DR. GIVINGS. Don't be alarmed.
Just lie down and relax.

She does.

DR. GIVINGS. Are you quite comfortable?

MRS. GIVINGS. Yes.

He holds the vibrator to her private parts, his face impassive.

DR. GIVINGS. Electricity is not to be feared – it is harnessed from nature. I remember, when I was a child, I was stroking the cat's back one day and was startled to see sparks rising up out of her fur. My father said, this is nothing but electricity, the same thing you see on the trees in a storm. My mother seemed alarmed. Stop stroking the cat. You might start a fire. I kept on stroking the cat. I thought: is nature a cat? If so, who strokes its back? God?*

MRS. GIVINGS. *(with some difficulty speaking)* And what did you determine?

DR. GIVINGS. Natural law.
Is that too much pressure?

MRS. GIVINGS. No.
Oh,
Oh,
Oh –
Kiss me, darling, kiss me.

DR. GIVINGS. Afterwards.

MRS. GIVINGS. No, kiss me now.
Kiss me and hold the instrument there, just there, at the same time.

DR. GIVINGS. Darling, no – that would be –

MRS. GIVINGS. I don't care, do it, do it, I have been longing to kiss someone. Like this.

She kisses him passionately and puts the vibrator back on her private parts.

DR. GIVINGS. This is what I feared. In a sick woman the device restores balance, but in a healthy woman it makes you excitable and perhaps even causes some perverse kind of onanism.

MRS. GIVINGS. What is onanism?

DR. GIVINGS. I am relieved that you do not know. I'm afraid the experiment was not a success dear.

MRS. GIVINGS. And I say it *was* a success! Kiss me, kiss me now!

He kisses her politely.

MRS. GIVINGS. This is inadequate! You are inadequate! Oh, God!

She has not yet had a paroxysm.
He takes the vibrator away from her.

DR. GIVINGS. I made a terrible mistake bringing you into the operating theater. Men of science should never mix their family lives and their medical lives. It was my mistake, my darling, and we will both forget about it.

He unplugs the vibrator.

DR. GIVINGS. Now I want you to go upstairs and take a nap.

MRS. GIVINGS. No!

DR. GIVINGS. Catherine.

She dresses and Dr. Givings helps her with innumerable buttons

MRS. GIVINGS. I shall take a walk. Will you help me on with this – *for God's sake why does it have so many buttons?*

DR. GIVINGS. There *are* quite a lot of buttons.

MRS. GIVINGS. I could walk walk walk all night in the snow.

DR. GIVINGS. Is it snowing out?

MRS. GIVINGS. You didn't notice the first snow? My God. When I first met you and was nothing more than a girl I wrote my name in the snow outside your window – I

MRS. GIVINGS. *(cont.)*would have done anything for you to notice me – you were older, and seemed so wise, so calm – and so marvelously indifferent to me. I don't know if you ever saw it – it melted – no matter, if you saw my name in the snow all you'd see was a natural substance –

DR. GIVINGS. Catherine.

MRS. GIVINGS. I'm afraid you've done up the buttons wrong.

DR. GIVINGS. Sorry.

He starts doing the buttons over again.

MRS. GIVINGS. It was an unnecessary gesture, childish, a name in the snow, but a gift must be unnecessary – for it to be good – but you want it to be *useful,* you wouldn't say – well, it's useless – but you made it for me alone. And so it will never melt. It will exist for all time. Uuugh – how ridiculous I sound. My hat please.

She is dressed.

DR. GIVINGS. I made a very bad mistake today and I am sorry.

He tries to touch her.

MRS. GIVINGS. Good-bye!

She leaves the operating theater
She leaves the house without her coat, hat or mittens.

DR. GIVINGS. Take your wrap! It's cold!
Did you really write your name in the snow?

Dr. Givings, alone.
He washes up, resigned.
He splahses his face with water.
He looks at the water,
and becomes entranced.
Fascinated, inspired.

DR. GIVINGS. Annie!

Annie appears.

DR. GIVINGS. Can you take this down? I have suddenly thought up a new invention.

She takes notes.

DR. GIVINGS. A vibrator made of water! The healing power of water, married to a great electrical force – could be – my goodness, revolutionary. The patient would experience a *calming* effect from the water, even as she has a release from the pressure, revitalizing the circulation. It could be used on patients who are prone to excitability – like my wife – that is to say – we will need twenty feet of copper piping right away, can you order it from the hardware store as soon as possible?

ANNIE. Yes, sir.

Annie exits.
Dr. Givings tries to work out with his
hands in the air how his invention would work.
Mrs. Givings re-enters the living room with Leo.
They are laughing and their faces are flushed.

MRS. GIVINGS. How glad I am that I found you!

LEO. And I you.

You might have caught a terrible fever making snow angels without your coat – you looked like a fallen angel.

MRS. GIVINGS. Did I? Oh, I am cold, but the cold feels marvelous, I feel awake, my skin is tingling.

LEO. I must paint you like this.

MRS. GIVINGS. Leo – Mr. Irving – I must ask you – I know it is not proper – but I do not care today, I do not care at all – when you receive the treatment from my husband, where does he put it? The instrument?

LEO. I do not think your husband would like me to say, he would only speak of it in Latin or in Greek.

MRS. GIVINGS. Well, I only know English. Can you show me on my person?

LEO. Er – no. I may be an artist but I am also a gentleman.

MRS. GIVINGS. There is no such thing. Which is it, Mr. Irving? Do you dare to be an artist, or a gentleman?

She moves towards him.

He moves away.

LEO. Look at the snow, out the window. Do you not think, Mrs. Givings, that snow is always kind? Because it has to fall slowly, to meet the ground slowly, or the eyelash slowly – And things that meet each other slowly are kind.

MRS. GIVINGS. You are changing the subject.

LEO. Indeed I am.

MRS. GIVINGS. Meet me slowly, like snow.

She puts her hand on his cheek, slowly.

MRS. GIVINGS. I cannot bear it.

Dr. Givings enters, yelling for Annie.

DR. GIVINGS. Wait – Annie – we'll also need ten copper valves –

He sees his wife's hand on Leo's cheek.

Had a good walk I trust?

Mrs. Givings takes her hand from Leo's cheek.
She says nothing.

LEO. I discovered your wife in the snow with no coat and insisted upon walking her home to warm her up before she caught a fever.

DR. GIVINGS. Then you did me a very great service, Mr. Irving.

LEO. Good-bye, Dr. Givings, Mrs. Givings.

DR. GIVINGS. Good-bye.

Dr. Givings turns to his wife.

DR. GIVINGS. Was your hand on his cheek?

MRS. GIVINGS. It was.

DR. GIVINGS. I see.

MRS. GIVINGS. And do you mind very much?

A pause, he considers.

DR. GIVINGS. It is odd – for some husbands such things end in a screaming match or even in death, one hand on a cheek. It has come to mean an absolute thing: the end of a book, those dreadful Mrs. Bovary books – but how can it be absolute when there are so many shades and degrees of love? Lady novelists like for it to be a tragedy – because it means that the affair mattered, mattered terribly – but it doesn't, it needn't.

MRS. GIVINGS. The writer of Madame Bovary was not a woman.

DR. GIVINGS. He was French, which is much the same thing.

MRS. GIVINGS. You dare to make a joke about the French – at this moment? Most men would be – pale with rage!

DR. GIVINGS. Pale with rage, exactly, in a sentimental novel. My point is: this is not the end of the book. You made a mistake, that is all. The treatment I gave you made you excitable. It is my fault. A hand on the cheek, these are muscles, skin, facts. It needn't mean that one is preferred absolutely, or that one isn't loved. So why then jealousy? My darling, I don't mind.

MRS. GIVINGS. Oh.

I had hoped that you would mind.

She stomps out of the room.
Dr. Givings is left there, alone.

DR. GIVINGS. Catherine?

He follows after her.

MRS. GIVINGS. Don't talk to me tonight, don't talk to me tomorrow! I will take breakfast in my own room!

A door slamming.
A song on the piano.

Second Scene

A few days later.
Leo is painting Elizabeth, who is nursing Letitia.
She is dressed vaguely as the Virgin Mary, in one of
Mrs. Giving's gowns.
Mrs. Givings watches Leo paint.
The painting does not face us, we do not see it.

LEO. It will be a revolution! I will call it: Nursing Madonna! How can there be so few Madonnas in which the baby Jesus actually gives suck.

MRS. GIVINGS. We are to think of Him feeding us, I suppose. Not the other way round.

Mrs. Givings gets up and paces.
She is jealous, of nursing and of being painted.
Leo goes to Elizabeth.

LEO. *(to Elizabeth)* Elizabeth, could you just –

He arranges the fabric so that the breast is more exposed.
Mrs. Givings examines the painting.

MRS. GIVINGS. Hmm.

LEO. Don't look at it, it's not done yet –

MRS. GIVINGS. Sorry.

LEO. Elizabeth, could you just –

He angles her head toward the baby.

LEO. There. Beautiful. There is nothing so peaceful as nursing a baby. The baby and the mother become one being, do they not?

Mrs. Givings taps her foot.

LEO. You seem nervous, Mrs. Givings.

MRS. GIVINGS. We should stop. My husband will be home from the club shortly and he wouldn't approve of this, not at all.

LEO. I don't see why. Your husband is a man who understands science, why then he must understand nature.

Leo resumes painting.

MRS. GIVINGS. *(in low tones to Leo)* I am not supposed to talk to his patients, much less arrange for them to see the bare breasts of the – help – in my living room.

LEO. Leave behind the stranglehold of convention and loosen your corset, Mrs. Givings, you will breathe much better.

ELIZABETH. She is done eating. She has fallen asleep.

He paints.
Mrs. Givings paces.

MRS. GIVINGS. I can hold the baby.

LEO. I need her there for the angle of Elizabeth's hands.

MRS. GIVINGS. Oh.

What day of the week is it, anyway?

ELIZABETH. Wednesday.

MRS. GIVINGS. That's right, Wednesday. It is always Wednesday, isn't it? Or it was Wednesday only yesterday. It is almost never Friday. It is never, ever Tuesday, but always Wednesday, I find. Smack in the middle of the week. With nothing to look forward to but the charwoman coming and cleaning out the ashes.

Are you almost done with her hands?

LEO. Hands are difficult. You would think they would just be five quick lines, but no, they have personalities as intimate as faces. Elizabeth's hands, for instance – they are fine hands, with long fingers that remind me of tapered candles. A person one has loved – the memory of their hands. That is what I wish to express in my paintings. The memory – of the movement – of very particular hands, even though they appear to be unmoving on canvas.

MRS. GIVINGS. Have you loved many women, Mr. Irving? Do you remember many – hands?

LEO. I have loved enough women to know how to paint. If I had loved fewer, I would be an illustrator; if I had loved more, I would be a poet.

MRS. GIVINGS. Are poets required to love many women?

LEO. Oh, yes. Love animates every line.

MRS. GIVINGS. But what of the rest of us mere mortals. How many times must we fall in love in order to live through the week.

LEO. There is also the love of God, love of country, love of children.

MRS. GIVINGS. Indeed.

LEO. I must look at her hands.

The front door opens. He stops painting.
Dr. Givings enters.
They startle.
Elizabeth covers her breast.
Dr. Givings is shocked at the scene in his living room.
Then he pretends he hasn't seen anything.

DR. GIVINGS. You are early for your appointment, Mr. Irving.

LEO. Yes.

DR. GIVINGS. I will wash up and see you in the operating theater.

Good afternoon, Elizabeth. *Catherine.*

He exits to the operating theater.

ELIZABETH. Oh, God.

MRS. GIVINGS. It's all right. As you see, he is a man of science. Nothing upsets or shocks him.

LEO. You talk as if that's a crime. What a capital husband you have. Completely beyond the dictates of modern society. I love your husband.

ELIZABETH. Shall I take the baby into the nusery?

MRS. GIVINGS. Yes, that will be all, Elizabeth.

I will put the paint things away.

Go to your *appointment,* Mr. Irving.

LEO. Thank you, Elizabeth. You were nothing short of divine.

Did you mind terribly being looked at? Being seen?

ELIZABETH. Who minds being seen?

LEO. Who?

ELIZABETH. Only criminals. I suppose.

LEO. Indeed.

MRS. GIVINGS. Good-day, Mr. Irving.

LEO. Mrs. Givings.

Leo enters the operating theater.

DR. GIVINGS. No need to undress all the way. We can be quick about it. Just lower your trousers.

Meanwhile, Mrs. Givings tries to hide the painting.

DR. GIVINGS. It seems that you and my wife are becoming acquinated.

LEO. A bit.

DR. GIVINGS. I see. She's a wonderful woman, is she not?

LEO. Yes.

DR. GIVINGS. I'm a lucky man.

Dr. Givings inserts the Chattanooga vibrator, a little more firmly than usual.

DR. GIVINGS. And your health, it seems to be much improved?

LEO. Yes, I am painting again. In fact, I cannot stop painting.

DR. GIVINGS. How wonderful. I am so glad for you.

Leo has an anal paroxysm.

LEO. Oh.

DR. GIVINGS. I do think you're cured now.
We can stop the treatments.

LEO. Thank you, doctor.
I believe you've saved my life.

Dr. Givings puts away the vibrator.

LEO. I am suddenly drowsy.

DR. GIVINGS. Take a nap.
Good day.

In the living room,
The door-bell rings.
Mrs. Givings answers the door.
Mr. and Mrs. Daldry enter.

MRS. GIVINGS. Ah, Mr. and Mrs. Daldry!

MR. AND MRS. DALDRY. Hello.

MRS. GIVINGS. I have not visited with you since it was raining, Mr. Daldry.

MR. DALDRY. And I have not seen you since you were wet.

Have you been well?

You look well.

Very well.

MRS. GIVINGS. Thank you.

MR. DALDRY. It's good you're done with that odious nursing business. A woman like you should be – enjoying yourself – not shut up in a nursery all day.

MRS. DALDRY. *(to Mr. Daldry)* Will you do me a favor, my dear, and take a walk around the grounds before my appointment?

In the next room, Dr. Givings exits to his study. Leo drowses.

MRS. DALDRY. I wish to speak to Mrs. Givings about my needle-work before Dr. Givings arrives and I fear we'll bore you.

MR. DALDRY. I don't have much to say on the subject of needlepoint. I'll see you shortly. Darling. Mrs. Givings.

MRS. GIVINGS. *(as he moves to the door)* Take a left turn by the fountain – there is a winter garden – I planted it myself –

MR. DALDRY. I didn't know anything grew in winter –

MRS. GIVINGS. Oh, yes – juniper and periwinkle and –

MR. DALDRY. It's all the same to me. But if you planted it, Mrs. Givings, I'm sure it's lovely.

He exits.

MRS. DALDRY. I wanted to speak with you.

MRS. GIVINGS. Come and sit. You have taken up needle-work?

MRS. DALDRY. No. I hate needle-work. I have been thinking about what you said –

about having two experiences of the same event.

I want very much to – I do not know how to –

but I was thinking – if we go into the operating theater again, and if we place the instrument just so – and if you held it, and then I held it – but we did a kind of –

She gestures, oddly.
Elizabeth enters.

ELIZABETH. I laid her down to sleep in her pram. I am sorry about the –

MRS. GIVINGS. Nevermind, Elizabeth. You may go now.

Wait, Elizabeth, before you leave –

perhaps you can settle a question.

Mrs. Daldry and I have had two experiences of the very same event.

Have you ever had this sensation?

Either: you have shivers all over your body, and you feel like running, and your feet get very hot, as though you are dancing on devil's coals –

MRS. DALDRY. Or you see unaccountable patterns of light, of electricity, under your eye-lids –

and your heart races – and your legs feel very weak, as though you cannot walk –

MRS. GIVINGS. Or your face gets suddenly hot, like a strange sudden sunburn –

MRS. DALDRY. Or there are red splotches up one side of your entire body – a strange rash – here –

(She points to her chest.)

MRS. GIVINGS. And the feeling of burning, as though you'll get no relief – and your mouth is dry and you have to lick your lips – and you find your face making a very ugly expression, so you cover your face with your hands –

MRS. DALDRY. And sometimes a great outpouring of liquid, and the sheets are wet, only it is not an unpleasant sensation, but a little frightening?

ELIZABETH. Is that a riddle?

MRS. GIVINGS. Has that ever happened to you?

ELIZABETH. I do not know – the sensations are so contradictory. Does anything unite them?

MRS. GIVINGS. Many of them are – down below.

ELIZABETH. Oh – I see.

Well, the things you describe, some of them seem to be sensations that an invalid would have, or someone with a horrible fever – but others – sound like sensations that women might have when they are having relations with their husbands.

A pause.

I'm sorry. Perhaps you were joking. Perhaps – I shouldn't have said –

MRS. GIVINGS. With their husbands?

MRS. DALDRY. How interesting.

ELIZABETH. Those sensations you are describing – they are not from having relations with your husbands?

MRS. DALDRY. Good heavens, no!

MRS. GIVINGS. No! Good God.

They laugh.

MRS. DALDRY. I don't know what I should do if I felt those things in the presence of my husband – I'd be so embarrassed I would leave the room immediately. As it is – my husband is very considerate – when he comes to my room at night, I am asleep – and he tells me to keep my eyes shut, and I do – so I feel only the darkness – and then the pain – I lie very still – I do not see his face – my husband is – has always been – very considerate.

MRS. GIVINGS. Of course.

MRS. DALDRY. But the instrument produces a very different kind of pain, does it not? Very different from the other kind of pain? With my husband –

Leo enters the room, a bit dazed.

LEO. Ladies.

> *They nod to him.*
> *Elizabeth is embarassed to see him.*

ELIZABETH. Good-bye then.

LEO. *(to Elizabeth)* I will see you home.
I have a good enough likeness, I can finish the painting at my studio.

ELIZABETH. I can walk home myself.

LEO. No, I wouldn't hear of it, I will walk you home.

ELIZABETH. No thank you, Mr. Irving.

LEO. Please. You did me a great service today, I can at least see that you get home.

MRS. GIVINGS. *(to Leo)* Oh, don't go just yet!

LEO. I'll just see Elizabeth home. Oh, the painting!

MRS. GIVINGS. I'll get it. I will see you soon?

LEO. I'm afraid my treatments are at an end. I'm cured.

MRS. GIVINGS. But that's impossible!

> *Dr. Givings enters from the operating room*
> *and sees the good-bye between Leo and Catherine.*

LEO. I will see you again. Never fear. Good-bye, Catherine. *(He takes her hand, sees Dr. Givings, and drops it.)* Dr. Givings. Farewell.

DR. GIVINGS. Mrs. Daldry. I did not hear you arrive. I'll just let you get ready.

> *Mrs. Daldry moves to the operating room and undresses*
> *with the help of Annie. In the living room:*

DR. GIVINGS. What can you be thinking of? Do you mean to embarrass me?

MRS. GIVINGS. I thought it was only a scene in a book to you. Or a fact.

DR. GIVINGS. Do you think it's escaped my notice that you haven't breakfasted with me for five days running?

MRS. GIVINGS. Breakfast is not a very romantic meal. I decided to skip it.

DR. GIVINGS. Is every meal supposed to be romantic?

MRS. GIVINGS. I do not enjoy you silently reading your scientific journals while I eat my toast.

DR. GIVINGS. You prefer grand passions over toast? My God, woman, we are married, a man needs to be quiet at least once a day.

MRS. GIVINGS. So I'll be quiet then! HERE I AM! QUIET! QUIET AS A MOUSE!

Mr. Daldry enters the living room.

MR. DALDRY. What a beautiful winter garden – sorry, am I interrupting?

MRS. GIVINGS. No. We were just discussing breakfast. You know, in Italy they hardly eat breakfast. Just a little bit of sweet cracker to dip in very strong coffee. They eat something light to recover from the great passions they spent during the night. Better to skip breakfast and move onto lunch, a great big lunch, when the the silence isn't quite so loud, no the silence is not quite so deafening at lunch.

DR. GIVINGS. How do you know about biscotti?

MRS. GIVINGS. Mr. Irving told me.

DR. GIVINGS. I see.

MR. DALDRY. I know nothing about biscotti. I like ham and eggs for breakfast, sausage too. A big breakfast is important for one's energy, Mrs. Givings. I have once heard it said that small women should eat large animals. You ought to eat a bit of meat for breakfast, some bacon, or some sausage.

MRS. GIVINGS. Oh, I have plenty of energy, Mr. Daldry. I don't need to borrow energy from a cow. I have so much energy I do not know what to do with it, you see.

MR. DALDRY. Mmmm.

Annie sticks her head in the living room:

ANNIE. We're ready for you, doctor.

DR. GIVINGS. Will you excuse me.

MRS. GIVINGS & MR. DALDRY. *(an approximation of)*
Oh, yes, certainly.

Dr. Givings enters the operating theater.
He is distracted.
He puts the vibrator on Mrs. Daldry's torso.

MRS. DALDRY. Dr. Givings?

DR. GIVINGS. Yes?

MRS. DALDRY. Is something wrong?

DR. GIVINGS. Oh – terribly sorry. I am distracted.

He moves the vibrator.
Meanwhile, Mr. Daldry and Mrs. Givings sit.
He moves towards her.

MR. DALDRY. Mrs. Givings. I – don't always know how to converse – in a drawing room. I –

He tries to kiss her.
She slaps him.

MRS. GIVINGS. Mr. Daldry!

DR. GIVINGS. Here? Is this better?

MRS. GIVINGS. What can you be thinking of?

MR. DALDRY. You said about your energies. I thought –

MRS. GIVINGS. You insult me.

MR. DALDRY. You have no idea how I long for a woman of energy. My wife is so tired, she is so tired, all the time.

MRS. GIVINGS. How dare you speak ill of your wife in my presence. Go. Please.

MR. DALDRY. Will you have the goodness to tell Mrs. Daldry to meet me at home, I will send a carriage for her.

Mrs. Givings nods.
He leaves.
She goes to the door of the operating theater and hesitates there, sinking down, upset.

DR. GIVINGS. It has been taking longer with you of late. Perhaps I need to build a new instrument with a few more beats per minute – perhaps the body gets accustomed to so many beats per minute and then requires more –

He adjusts the vibrator.

Hmm. Nothing. Is it past three minutes?

He looks at his pocket watch.

MRS. DALDRY. Perhaps if Annie tries.

DR. GIVINGS. Yes, of course, Annie why don't you have a go. I will attend to some business.

Annie takes the vibrator and tries.
Dr. Givings leaves the room.
He almost trips on his wife who is listening at the door.

DR. GIVINGS. My God. You are acting the part of a madwoman in a play!
Listening at doors?

MRS. GIVINGS. You will offer to her what you deny to me!

DR. GIVINGS. It is *medicine,* my love!

MRS. GIVINGS. And I say it isn't!

DR. GIVINGS. I thought I heard a slap!

MRS. GIVINGS. It was nothing, nothing at all.

Mrs. Daldry has a louder than usual paroxysm.
They both hear it.

MRS. GIVINGS. Well, your work is done now.
You can go to the club.
And argue about the benefits of the alternating current over and above the direct current.

DR. GIVINGS. And you?
Do you favor the alternating or direct?

MRS. GIVINGS. Direct. From here to here.

She gestures from his heart to her heart.

DR. GIVINGS. Interesting. I would have guessed alternating. More complicated, changing direction dozens of times per second. Faces slapped by nobody. Italian breakfasts. Etcetera. I'll be at the club.

He exits.
Mrs. Givings moves towards the operating theater.
Annie and Mrs. Daldry are sitting in a weirdly compromised
post-coital state of reflection.

MRS. DALDRY. Annie, have you ever used the instrument upon yourself?

ANNIE. Oh, no. For I've never been ill. I've scarcely had a day's illness in my life. Maybe a bit of a stomach bug, but nothing mental. I'm sound as a horse, I was raised on a farm.

MRS. DALDRY. I could hold the instrument on you, if you would like, it is not unpleasant, and perhaps it would be interesting for you to experience it.

ANNIE. I do not think the doctor would like it.

Mrs. Givings enters the operating theater.

MRS. GIVINGS. My husband has gone to the club. And Mr. Daldry has also left. He sent a carriage for you. They both said their farewells.

MRS. DALDRY. Thank you, Mrs. Givings.

MRS. GIVINGS. Shall I leave you?

I could –

A suspended moment in which
we are not sure if we might witness
three women playing with the vibrator together.
All of them think about it.
They all look at one another, and then at the instrument.

MRS. DALDRY. I –

ANNIE. I –

MRS. DALDRY. I must get dressed.

MRS. GIVINGS. Of course. Annie, do you need any assistance cleaning up?

ANNIE. No, thank you, Mrs. Givings. It's very easy to clean up.

MRS. GIVINGS. All right then.

I will leave you.

Mrs. Givings exits.
Annie helps Mrs. Daldry get dressed.

MRS. DALDRY. Well.

ANNIE. Well, then.

MRS. DALDRY. I suppose we could – continue with my Greek lesson.

ANNIE. Oh, yes. I believe we left off with the early Greek philosophers. Thales thought the earth was suspended on water, floated there, and he thought that all magnets had souls because they moved towards one another.

MRS. DALDRY. I can well believe that magnets have souls. When I look into dark eyes, like magnets, I am moved, unaccountably. You have very dark eyes, like magnets– has any man ever told you so?

ANNIE. No man has told me much aside from: pass the clamp.

MRS. DALDRY. They should Annie, they really should. Whatever happened to Thales?

ANNIE. He never married. His mother told him he should marry and he said: It's too early. And when she pressed him again, ten years later, he said: It's too late.

MRS. DALDRY. And you? Why have you never married?

ANNIE. One day, I woke up, and it was too late.

MRS. DALDRY. I see. Annie, I have been thinking. I wonder whether I could purchase one of these instruments for home use. The doctor is so busy, and I really feel I'm almost better. My color has returned, and I wake up in the morning and feel hopeful. I could use it only as required, when, for example, I have trouble sleeping, as I often do, and I can't very well call on the doctor past midnight.

ANNIE. Well – it might be dangerous for home use, because of the potential for electrocution, but I will ask the doctor. You know he is very open to inventions.

MRS. DALDRY. I would be too embarassed to ask.

ANNIE. I will ask for you.

MRS. DALDRY. Good-bye then, Annie.

ANNIE. Good-bye.

MRS. DALDRY. Thank you, Annie.

ANNIE. For what?

MRS. DALDRY. For the Greek lesson.

> *Mrs. Daldry exits.*
> *Annie washes her hands.*
> *She looks at the vibrator, thinks of using it on herself,*
> *thinks better of it, puts it away.*
>
> *Meanwhile, Mrs. Givings is lying on the sofa in the*
> *living room.*

MRS. DALDRY. Are you quite all right, Mrs. Givings? Your color looks off.

MRS. GIVINGS. I am not myself.

MRS. DALDRY. Is there anything I can do?

MRS. GIVINGS. No, thank you.

Mrs. Daldry, did you dream of love from a young age?

MRS. DALDRY. Yes.

MRS. GIVINGS. And what did you think it would be like?

MRS. DALDRY. I thought it would be – never wanting for anything. Being surrounded and lifted up. Like resting on water, for eternity.

MRS. GIVINGS. And is that what you have found in marriage?

MRS. DALDRY. There have been moments of rest. But as it turns out, the earth rests on air, not on water, and the air can feel very – insubstantial – at times. Even though it is holding you up, invisibly.

MRS. GIVINGS. Yes.

MRS. DALDRY. Do you mind if I play your piano?

MRS. GIVINGS. Oh, please do.

> *Mrs. Daldry plays the piano, full of longing.*
> *From off stage, the baby cries.*

MRS. GIVINGS. Excuse me.

Mrs. Givings exits to attend to the baby.
Annie enters and listens to Mrs Daldry play.
Annie goes to sit beside Mrs. Daldry on the piano bench.
Mrs. Daldry finishes the song.
Annie claps.
They kiss.

MRS. DALDRY. What?

ANNIE. Oh.

MRS. DALDRY. How strange.

ANNIE. Oh dear.

MRS. DALDRY. I had better not see you ever again.

ANNIE. I suppose not.

MRS. DALDRY. Good-bye then Annie.

ANNIE. Good-bye.

Mrs. Daldry exits.
Mrs. Givings enters.

MRS. GIVINGS. Annie?

ANNIE. What a sad song she played. I believe it made me tear up a little. Good-bye Mrs. Givings.

MRS. GIVINGS. Oh, don't leave Annie, Dr. Givings is at the club and I have very little company.

ANNIE. I'm afraid I must go.

MRS. GIVINGS. What is the matter?

ANNIE. That song made me sad. Good-bye.

Mrs. Givings, alone.
The door-bell rings.
Elizabeth enters, not entirely herself.

MRS. GIVINGS. Elizabeth. I did not expect you. What is it?

ELIZABETH. Mrs. Givings, I came to tell you that today was my last day working for you. My husband doesn't like me gone so much. He wants me home with my own children.

MRS. GIVINGS. But you can't leave us, Elizabeth! What on earth will we do without you?

ELIZABETH. She is almost ready to have cow's milk. Or a little bit of rice porridge.

MRS. GIVINGS. I suppose. I was not thinking only of the food.

Elizabeth nods slowly.

MRS. GIVINGS. But why today? I don't understand.

ELIZABETH. Mr. Irving insisted on walking me home. He was not – inappropriate – but he kept hold of my arm. He paid me a large sum of money – for the sitting. And he walked me up to my front door.

MRS. GIVINGS. Oh, dear.

ELIZABETH. My husband was home. My husband saw him. And me. And the painting.

MRS. GIVINGS. Oh! Was your husband very angry? About the painting?

ELIZABETH. The painting? No. He cried when he saw the painting. It's your hands, he said. Mr. Irving must be a good painter, it's hard to paint hands.
But he doesn't want me working here, not anymore.

MRS. GIVINGS. Of course. Yes – I understand.

ELIZABETH. No – you don't.

A pause

ELIZABETH. I'll just say good-bye to Lotty. I have grown fond of her.

MRS. GIVINGS. Yes. Well.
She is in the nursery. She is fat and happy, all thanks to you.
Elizabeth – how old was your Henry Douglas when he died?

ELIZABETH. Twelve weeks.

MRS. GIVINGS. What did he die of?

ELIZABETH. Cholera.

MRS. GIVINGS. I am sorry.

ELIZABETH. Thank you.

MRS. GIVINGS. I think I should die of sorrow, in your place.

ELIZABETH. Die of sorrow? A mother of two cannot die of sorrow.

MRS. GIVINGS. But how do you go on, after?

ELIZABETH. My mother told me to pray each day since I was a little girl, to pray that you borrow everything, everyone you love, from God. That way your heart doesn't break when you have to give your son, or your mother, or your husband, back to God. I prayed Jesus, let me be humble. I borrowed my child, I borrowed my husband, I borrowed my own life from you, God. But he felt like mine not like God's he felt like mine more mine than anything.

God must have this huge horrible cabinet – all the babies who get returned – and all those babies inside, they're all crying even with God Himself to rock them to sleep, still they want their mothers. So when I started to feel something for this baby, for your baby, I thought no, take her back God.

When I first met her all I could think was: she is alive and Henry is not. I had all this milk – I wished it would dry up. Just get through the year, I thought. Your milk will dry up and you will forget. The more healthy your baby got, the more dead my baby became. I thought of her like a tic. I thought – fill her up and then pop! You will see the blood of my Henry underneath. But she seemed so grateful for the milk. Sometimes I hated her for it. But she would look at me, she would give me this look – I do not know what to call it if it is not called love. I hope every day you keep her – you keep her close to you – and you remember the blood that her milk was made from. The blood of my son, my Henry. Good-bye, Mrs. Givings.

MRS. GIVINGS. Good-bye, Elizabeth.

Elizabeth nods.

Mrs. Givings touches Elizabeth's elbow.

Elizabeth pulls away and exits, to the nursery.

MRS. GIVINGS. Thank you.

> *But Elizabeth is out the door.*
> *Mrs. Givings, alone.*
> *She moves toward the operating theater.*
> *The door-bell rings.*
> *It is Leo.*

MRS. GIVINGS. You have made quite a mess of things for Elizabeth.

LEO. I know. I'm sorry. I've come to say good-bye.

I'm moving to Paris.

MRS. GIVINGS. When?

LEO. Tomorrow.

MRS. GIVINGS. Take me with you.

LEO. Are you out of your mind?

MRS. GIVINGS. You are surprised? It was you who seduced me!

LEO. What?

MRS. GIVINGS. All that talk of women, two thirds done, that was me, you were talking of me, were you not?

LEO. I was talking of paintings. I –

MRS. GIVINGS. No one has ever spoken to me of those things before. Of beauty – of prostitutes, of – my God, of Italy. How could I have misunderstood your intentions? I'm in love with you.

LEO. Oh, dear Catherine I am afraid I cannot love you. If there is any type to whom I am attracted – it veers toward women with doe eyes. And your eyes are more – they are more – thin – the light bounces off them rather than into them. And I cannot see your soul hovering here, where I would like to. Your soul is locked somewhere inside your body, so I cannot see it. Another man could perhaps bring your soul outside your eyes but it's not me, I'm afraid. I do care for you though.

MRS. GIVINGS. Try. Try to bring my soul out – to here. If you look into my eyes – see – I will try.

Are you bringing another woman with you?

LEO. No – I am going alone.

Don't you see? It is Elizabeth who I love.

MRS. GIVINGS. Elizabeth?

LEO. Yes.

MRS. GIVINGS. Oh – I see nothing, I understand nothing – my God, Elizabeth.

LEO. Yes. And she doesn't care for me, not at all, I told her of my affections on our walk and she slapped me. No– I will go to Paris alone. I am married to my solitude.

MRS. GIVINGS. I can be your solitude. I will be quiet as a mouse. I understand solitude, I am very lonely.

LEO. I do not understand your loneliness, Mrs. Givings. You have a child, a husband – a home!

MRS. GIVINGS. Yes. I am very ungrateful. I am sure that God will punish me.

She tries to embrace him.

LEO. No. You do not love me. You only think you do. You love your husband. He is a good man. Good-bye, now.

He kisses her hands.

MRS. GIVINGS. Elizabeth is in the nursery. If you wish to say good-bye to her.

LEO. I can't bear to see her. Just give her this, won't you?

Leo kisses Mrs. Givings on the cheek.

Come visit me in France. I promise you – you'll love the paintings.

He leaves.
She goes into the operating theater.
She plugs in the vibrator.
She puts it to her private parts but
she is too sad for it to work.
She cries as it hums along.
Dr. Givings enters.

DR. GIVINGS. My dear, what on earth are you doing?

MRS. GIVINGS. *(bawling)* I am alone.

DR. GIVINGS. You are not alone, I am here. Have you been using this instrument on yourself?

Dr. Givings shuts off the vibrator.

MRS. GIVINGS. I am so lonely – Elizabeth is leaving us – Leo is leaving us – everyone is leaving – you are gone – you are at the club, or in the next room, always in the next room, with the door locked. You see that women are capable of pressing a button themselves.

DR. GIVINGS. Darling –

MRS. GIVINGS. When you touched them, the other women, and Leo, with the machine, did you feel love for them, when you touched them there, was it like love?

DR. GIVINGS. No. I only wanted them to feel better.

MRS. GIVINGS. And when you married me, did you want to love me, or did you want to make me feel better?

DR. GIVINGS. A doctor wants to make everyone feel better.

MRS. GIVINGS. But did you want to love me?

DR. GIVINGS. Yes! And you – with your hands on other men's faces – do you love them? Do you love Mr. Irving?

MRS. GIVINGS. A little.

DR. GIVINGS. I have a strange feeling in my stomach.

MRS. GIVINGS. What is it?

DR. GIVINGS. My eyes feel funny and my stomach feels jumpy. I believe I'm jealous.

MRS. GIVINGS. Give up your operating theater, darling.

DR. GIVINGS. And do what instead?

MRS. GIVINGS. Love me. Love me for your job.

DR. GIVINGS. All day long?

MRS. GIVINGS. All day long. I have heard that some women do not need the vibrating instrument to give them paroxysms, that relations with their husbands have much the same effect. Love me for your job.

DR. GIVINGS. I would like to love you.

MRS. GIVINGS. Would you?

DR. GIVINGS. Yes. I have not known how.

MRS. GIVINGS. You said to me when my hand was on another man's cheek that there were all types and shades of love – But what is it then, this very particular way in which you love me? What color? What temperature? And please do not say: you are my wife, I am your husband.

DR. GIVINGS. I do not have the words.

MRS. GIVINGS. Please try.

DR. GIVINGS. That is why they have poets – to classify all the degrees of love. It is for scientists to classify the maladies arising from the want of it.

MRS. GIVINGS. Try.

DR. GIVINGS. Do not make fun of me. Do you promise?

MRS. GIVINGS. I promise.

DR. GIVINGS. *(kissing tenderly each place as he names it – they are all on the face)*

I bless thee: temporomandibular joint

I bless thee: buccal artery and nerve

I bless thee: depressor anguli oris

I bless thee: zygomatic arch

I bless thee: temporalis fascia.

I bless thee, Catherine.

Mrs. Givings cries, it is so intimate.

MRS. GIVINGS. Open me.

DR. GIVINGS. Here?

MRS. GIVINGS. Away from the machine.

In the garden.

Undress me there.

DR. GIVINGS. You wish to undress in the garden in December?

MRS. GIVINGS. Yes, and please,

do not call me impractical. Our whole

future happiness depends upon it.

Dr. and Mrs. Givings kiss.
Although the domestic space seemed terribly permanent–
a settee, a statuette– suddenly it disappears and we are
in a sweet small winter garden. Snow covers trees that in
the spring flower with pink flowers.

MRS. GIVINGS. Undress me.

Do not close your eyes, look at me...

He undresses her, partially.

DR. GIVINGS. The street lamps are coming on. Someone will see us.

MRS. GIVINGS. No one will see. They are not electric yet.

Thank God something still flickers.

She undresses him.

MRS. GIVINGS. Are you cold?

DR. GIVINGS. No. Are you cold?

MRS. GIVINGS. No.

We don't need to see all of his body,
it is dark out—
but we do see the moon glowing off his skin,
off his back and shoulders.
He need not face us.
She has never seen him naked before—
she has only seen him under the covers.

MRS. GIVINGS. How beautiful you are! Your body!

I have never before seen that little bit there, under the covers –

or that bit there, or this beautiful line here –

I have felt this shadow there but I have never seen it –

how it curves –

Pointing to different lines on his body.

DR. GIVINGS. I am embarrassed.

MRS. GIVINGS. Don't be.

Lie down and make a snow angel.

He lies on his back and makes an angel in the snow.
She lies on top of him.
They make an angel.
They make their wings go back and forth.
It snows on them.
Outside, on the street corners,
the gas lamps go on, one by one,
flickering, insubstantial.

DR. GIVINGS. Catherine.

MRS. GIVINGS. Oh, God. Oh, God, Oh God.

And the rest of the lights go out.
The end.

Acknowledgements

I would like to thank New Dramatists and some wonderful actors who helped me in the workshop phase of this play: Eisa Davis, Carla Harting, Reed Birney, Mary Catherine Garrison, Michael Esper, Amy Warren, Marin Ireland, and the whole cast of Eurydice. Thanks to Kathleen Chalfant for loaning us her living room when we read the very first draft of this play. Thank you to Andre Bishop and Bernie Gersten for believing the play could survive on Broadway. Thanks to all the designers—Annie, David, Russell, Bray and Jonathan for being genius collaborators. Thank you to Paula Vogel, Anne Cattaneo, Madeline Oldham and Denise Bilbao for reading early drafts; and to Tina Howe, Kathleen Tolan, Andy Bragen, Crystal Finn, Kate Pines, Sarah Rasmussen, Roy Harris, Denise Yaney, Vanessa Poggioli, and David Adjmi for helping me get through previews. And many many thanks to Les Waters, without whom this play would never have been written, and to the original cast in Berkeley— Paul (also for your generosity revisiting the play), Hannah, Joaquin, Maria, Stacy, John, and Melle—for so bravely finding the play's voice. And to the cast at the Lyceum—Laura, Michael, Maria, Chandler, Tom, Quincy, Wendy—some of my favorite moments of theater were simply watching you all rehearse.

Also by
Sarah Ruhl...

The Clean House

Dead Man's Cell Phone

Eurydice

Please visit our website **samuelfrench.com** for complete
descriptions and licensing information

Breinigsville, PA USA
03 August 2010
242928BV00004B/1/P

OTHER TITLES AVAILABLE FROM SAMUEL FRENCH

DEAD MAN'S CELL PHONE

Sarah Ruhl

Dramatic Comedy / 2m, 4f / Unit Set

An incessantly ringing cell phone in a quiet café. A stranger at the next table who has had enough. And a dead man—with a lot of loose ends. So begins *Dead Man's Cell Phone*, a wildly imaginative new comedy by MacArthur "Genius" Grant recipient and Pulitzer Prize finalist, Sarah Ruhl, author of *The Clean House* and *Eurydice*. A work about how we memorialize the dead—and how that remembering changes us—it is the odyssey of a woman forced to confront her own assumptions about morality, redemption, and the need to connect in a technologically obsessed world.

"Satire is her oxygen. . . . In her new oddball comedy, *Dead Man's Cell Phone*, Sarah Ruhl is forever vital in her lyrical and biting takes on how we behave."
– *The Washington Post*

"Ruhl's zany probe of the razor-thin line between life and death delivers a fresh and humorous look at the times we live in."
– *Variety*

"[Ruhl] tackles big ideas with a voice that entertains"
– *NPR*

"…beguiling new comedy…Ms. Ruhl's work blends the mundane and the metaphysical, the blunt and the obscure, the patently bizarre and the bizarrely moving."
– *The New York Times*